TALK:
A NOVEL IN DIALOGUE

by

Corey Mesler

Livingston Press
at
The University of West Alabama

copyright © 2002 Corey Mesler

ISBN 0-942979-85-0, Hardcover
ISBN 0-942979-86-9, Quality Paperback

Library of Congress Number: 2001099093

This book is printed on paper that meets or exceeds
the Library of Congress's minimal standards
for acid-free paper.

Printed in the United States of America by:
United Graphics Incorporated

Hardcover binding by: Heckman Bindery

Typesetting: Sheletha Ross
Proofreaders: Robin Allen, Julian Tyler, Jodi Buckman,
Gina Montarsi, Heather Loper, Terri Barbour, Jody Hightower
Cover Art: Our grateful acknowledgment to Tim Crowder
for "Too Much Nothing To Say" (front) & "Duckus Ruckus" (back)
Cover Design: Joe Taylor

For Cheryl and Steve,
Tim and Eddie,
all great deipnosophists

Author's Hedge: This is a work of fiction. It is so fictive that it barely exists on our conscious plane. It is a work of the imagination, albeit a leaky one. The protagonist of the book is not me, nor is any character, large or small, described or named, based on anyone in the real world, living or dead. Even names that may sound similar to actual peoples's names do not connote—or denote—those individuals. Nothing in here is true. The author is a liar.

Acknowledgments: A portion of this appeared in slightly different form, as "This Party," in *Southern Voices*, an audio magazine edited by David Tankersley. The epigraph opening the book comes from Robert Musil's *The Man Without Qualities*, courtesy of Random House, Inc.

TALK:
A NOVEL IN DIALOGUE

1.

"We have all got to exert ourselves a little to keep sane, and call things by the same names other people call them by."

George Eliot
from *Middlemarch*

—Sit down and listen to me for a second.

—All right.

—I'm reviewing here. Looking at my life with an objective eye.

—Sounds dangerous.

—Sarcasm to a minimum please.

—Sorry.

—So I've figured out, this is as good as it gets.

—Really.

—Really.

—As good as it gets.

—Yes. I mean, look at me, I never thought I'd have all this, you know? Ok, the job is just right for me, a perfect fit, a match for my own personal mixture of ambition and desuetude. I'm just lazy enough to want it good without working too hard and this seems about right, ok, selling books, I'm good at it, I mean, I have some small reputation for being good at it, you know?

So money is ok, not great God knows, but I've got a house and I never thought I'd own a house, I mean, c'mon, when we were younger and floundering around and spending our Saturday nights with each other, feeling sorry for ourselves and gazing into our reflections in the rings under our glasses at the P&H, who thought we'd even do this, right?

—Mm hm.

—Ok, so I've surprised myself in this regard. A small life and a comfortable one. And there's the wife, no qualification needed. This is love, and pity the man who's never felt it when it's right, who doesn't have it as good. You know. Dorothea is everything, talk about perfect matches. She's strong, reliable, beautiful, honest, smart—

—Everything you're not.

—Thanks. But yeah. Like Rocky says, we fill gaps. And seven years down the road I'm still nuts about her and this is a remarkable thing. Still turned on by her, still watching the pivot of her hips, longing for a glance at her instep, the way she cocks her head. Really nice, really nice. And not what I expected when I was younger and supercilious, love lasting. It seemed pretty shoddy stuff to me when I was running through sequential relationships like ticking names off a list. Not fun, not healthy, though I regret little. But love lasting? Couldn't prove it by this cowboy. So I stand a little in awe of my marriage, just a little.

—Well you should.

—Thank you. You haven't done so poorly either. But to continue: the kids, c'mon. They break my heart. I couldn't have done a superior job, though I take little credit for their inherent wonderfulness. Someone decided to make both of them better than the sum of their parts. And joy, Lord. Watching them, listening to them, that's as good as life gets, eh? Both so full of marvels, both so *interesting*, you know?

—Oh, yeah. You know I love 'em.

—Thanks, yes, I do. God, they're beautiful. And this is love, you know? I mean no one who doesn't parent, if I can use that as a verb, knows what total, all-giving love can be, heart-rending, life-enhancing, soul-deep—

—Keep going.

—Heh. Ok. Point is I know all this. Self-knowledge for once paying off in spades. I *know* it. And I'm sitting in the lap of luxury, you know? I mean, I could use a little more money, would feel better not living from paycheck to paycheck, sure. But I gotta give myself some credit here—and you know that's not easy for me—I did all right. I did better than I thought I would and how many of us can say that, or how many of us know that? Hell, I've even got a nice car now, a big roomy dependable Honda van which Dorothea disparages as a soccer mom car. Is this where I thought I'd be in my early forties? God, even my dog, what a great dog. Even my dog, my wonderful border collie *fits*: smart, trouble-free, eager to please Flydog. I mean, really. The freaking lap of luxury, heaven, blissdom.

—But.

—Well, that's just it, right? The pressure. The coercion of all this good life: I *must* be happy. And I am, I am. So why am I so batty? Why are my nerves stretched taut? Why is every day a struggle just to keep myself pointed forward? Why am I as nervous as a cat, just this close to a full-blown panic attack, even alone in my home, just me and my thousands of books and my VCR and an old black and white movie to watch? Why should I be suffering the slings and arrows of outrageous contradiction, of deep-seeded depression in the face of bright sunshine? Hell is bad, but heaven, friend, is, I don't know, high pressure. You better be enjoying yourself.

—It's depression, pal, absolutely. You've had this before, it's a sickness, you know that, there's no shame in it. You could as easily have, oh, shingles.

—I know. I've been through it, yes, you were there. In the

hospital even.

—Yeah, you were sick, big deal, stop beating yourself up about it.

—I was sick. And it's like my body remembers it; it's body memory. I *feel* sick, queasy, nervous, rocky like I've got a flu all the time. Sometimes I feel like if I didn't have the responsibility, well, the love for my kids and wife, I don't know, I'd go ahead and have the nervous breakdown which is stalking me, creeping around the edges of my perimeter. My guilt about them protects me.

—Well, that's good, then.

—Is it?

—Were you happier when you were single and miserable and the flesh-loneliness made you want to cleave your own chest in two?

—No. I don't know. Not happier.

—Calmer?

—Yes. I was. Calmer, exactly.

—Hm.

—Yes, hm.

—I'm sorry, buddy. What can I do?

—Oh, no, nothing. I didn't mean that. What can you do? Nothing, nothing.

—Well, I would, as you know, um, do something, if I could.

—Yes.

—Maybe it's just age, you know? Maybe you handle, maybe one handles, different parts of life better. For some people it's youth, teen years. For some it's middle age. You're just having a tough time with middle age.

—Maybe.

—So where do we go from here?

—Exactly. Where?

—I don't know.

—And I don't know.

—Mm.

—Anyway. How about you? How are you?

—Don't ask.

*

—Hell, I worry about everything. The stories in the newspaper, the horror perpetrated daily, I can't even read some of the things they print, in graphic detail, just down the street, in sweet American suburbs, with kids, Jesus. What was it Saul Bellow said, there's nothing too rum to be true. He had that right. I mean I worry if a morning passes with my son and I didn't wring it for every meaningful glimmer of hope, as if every second I had to create a memory for him. That's tough, that's constant inner kicking. I worry what the neighbors think of me. I worry what my parents think of me. I worry if my son's friends don't come into the house and then, if they do, I worry about what they're doing. I worry if I've cooked our food long enough, or too long, I worry if my music's too loud, if I'm in the bath and the phone rings, if I answer the phone and it's a telemarketer I worry if I've given him or her enough grief, if I've missed an opportunity to punish them for their evil jobs. You know, I buy toilet paper—I can't seem to buy enough, I get the large economy size packages, my wife laughs, I can't get enough, you know, we always use it, it disappears no matter how much I buy—and what if I can't get to the store and buy some more, it's the finitude of things, what if we run out, I mean, I worry about that. I worry about the kids at school and daycare, remembering, really, my own woeful childhood and how neurotic I was and cried all through first grade. It doesn't matter that both my kids have more confidence than I ever had, that they glide where I skidded and crashed. It doesn't matter. I imagine their discomfort, fear, unhappiness and it's really all mine and I'm just projecting from my unstable school years all my own insecurities. You see, I know it and it doesn't stop the worrying. I worry about slighting people, people if it came right down to it, I don't care about one way or another, I worry about whether or not I slighted them, spoke too brusquely to them, didn't show enough interest in their conversation. Because I'm not interested. I'm not. I'm an egocentric ball of confusion and I don't listen to anybody else, but instead I worry that I don't listen to them and they can detect it and think me a boor or worse they get their feelings hurt. And Mogadishu, Sarajevo, Vietnam. Damn, I'm still worried about Vietnam. I missed that mess by a single year. My seventeenth birthday my lottery number was something like twenty-one. I mean the next year thank God they discontinued the draft but the worry remained, the anxiety accumulated in me somewhere like a calcium deposit or something and never left. Don't even let me think about my son becoming of draft age and there being some godawful conflict somewhere and I have to ponder his being in some man-made hell for years. Can't even think about it. And don't you love how they call it a "conflict." Jesus, as if war were reserved for more noble callings, the Big Ones. Isn't it warring if two countries are sending their young people against one another with high-powered weapons?

The military, shit, I worry about that too much. I mean, that's not even rational, is it? What's the military ever done to me? Just screwed with my psyche, just undermined my confidence in us as humans. But I've never really had to deal with them on a daily basis, not that I even could do it. Driving, crowds, being alone, crime, losing love, losing sexual interest, grocery shopping—I worry about grocery shopping. Sometimes I think the world is just too damned crowded with people, with activities, with words, with thoughts—too much damned stuff to think about. I worry that my mind can't even take it all in. It's like some preternatural setting in my subconscious was miscalculated and it left me unable to cope with the smallest of life's obstacles, something way back in the DNA setting. I'm predisposed to feel like shit about the modern world. Don't laugh. It's hell feeling like everyone else is coping, gliding through, not worrying about Mogadishu, or downtown LA, just buying their stereos and their video games and their pudding packs and not giving a second thought to how much dross the world is piling up, inside us and out. I know most everybody feels Ok about things, about each other even, but that just rubs me further, that just makes me feel worse. And I'm not the only one, the only one who is so stressed out by worldly stuff compounded by personal problems, but I'm more concerned with, how do those other guys do it? How do you *not* worry about whether the phone rings when you're in the bath, even if the machine will get it, even if it means only a few minutes lag time until you find out who called? How do they do it? The great unwashed masses who really make it all work, who keep the great machine oiled and running. I know I'm not doing my part, keeping my queer shoulder to the wheel. I know that somewhere along the line someone's gonna tap me on the shoulder and say, you're dead weight, man. The rest of us are doing our part.

What the hell are you doing? Where the hell have you been? I mean, I worry about that.

*

—You like Beefheart?

—You making lunch or putting some music on?

—Ha ha.

—Yeah, Beefheart, sure. I haven't listened to him in years, but whatever.

—Ok. So, what's going on?

—Nothing. I thought you called me.

—Right, right.

—You got something to discuss.

—Um, well, nothing new. You know, you're just—

—A sympathetic ear. What are you doing?

—I can't get this music loud enough. There. Nothing new, I just still, you know—

—Sure. You wanna hug?

—We don't hug.

—I know.

—So, this new girl at your work, she's, what, Katie or something.

—Katya.

—Oh. Foreign.

—In name anyway. What about her?

—She's good looking, yes?

—We're too old for the girl talk.

—Jesus, that doesn't leave us much to talk about. It's what we've always had, that heterosexual thing.

—That's us.

—She's cute, though, right?

—Yeah. In an Allie McBeal sort of way.

—That's in now.

—Yeah, she's in. She's way in. Would you leave the damn stereo alone? I can hear it.

—I know. You ever think that sometimes the same volume setting on the stereo dial doesn't always produce the same volume? Like sometimes the air is thicker or something and the sound just doesn't come out as loud.

—It's just different recording levels on different CDs. Some are louder than others, I don't know why.

—No, it's more than that. I know it is. Some days I have to turn the sucker way up just to get a good groove going. Other days it all comes out real heavy and you can hear every bass line and drum beat and the lyrics sound richer and you pick up on stuff you've never picked up on before. Those are good days.

—You're nuts, you know.

—That's what I've been worried about.

*

—Honey, you seen the Russian dressing?

—We don't have Russian dressing.

—We don't?

—We've never had Russian dressing. We don't like Russian dressing. What are you talking about?

—Don't you put Russian dressing on a Reuben?

—I don't know. You don't like Reubens.

—I don't? I thought I liked them.

—Have you ever had a Reuben?

—They have sauerkraut on them, right?

—I think so.

—I love them.

—Ok. Make yourself one then.

—I can't.

—We don't have any Russian dressing.

—Right.

*

—You know the other night, Dorothea rented another of Hollywood's big blockbusters and I was again amazed at how much outside the scheme of things I stand. They're not making movies for me anymore, that's plain.

—Whaddya see?

—*Jurassic Park.*

—I liked it.

—Everyone liked it. It's *ET* all over again. You know I see these things and I'm just agog at how nonsensical, how *a*sensical they are and how much they are loved and I think I'm going crazy. *Forrest Gump*, for Christ's sake. What a waste of time. A tale told by an idiot, Shakespeare didn't know how insipid that could be. I don't get it. I admit I don't get it.

—What was wrong with *Jurassic Park*?

—Oh, what was right? They don't bother to write stories. It's all just spectacle. Goddam Steven "Look at me" Spielberg, worst thing that ever happened to the movies.

—Don't start your Spielberg screed again.

—Ok, ok. But I mean talk about light with no heat. It's all so formulaic, so cookie cutter. The cute b-list actors, the roar, the lights, the over the top action action action, the sort of "you gotta find this entertaining" attitude, the fat guy from Seinfeld who gets all the roles now which used to go to the fat guy from Cheers.

—Whaddya long for, buddy?

—What do you mean?

—What nostalgic past are you mourning?

—Ok. You're humoring me. Your tone says get the guys with the white coats.

—No, really.

—Scripts, stories. *The Sweet Smell of Success.*

—Tony Curtis?

—Have you seen it?

—Actually, no. But I haven't really been tempted to.

—It's brilliant. It's everything these blockbusters today are not.

—You sound like our parents.

—Jesus, I know. But, what I'm mourning is my own sequestered sensibility, my own outside-the-ken artistic desires. I want a dialogue with the world, you know. I'm disconnected. I want to know I haven't been left behind in the general program of things, that there is still some art being produced that will appeal to me.

—Tall order.

—It isn't really, is it? Are you just kidding me?

*

—Book Shoppe. Hello?

—

—Oh, hi, honey.

—

—I'm leaving. Five minutes, five and a half. Maybe better say five minutes and 45 seconds.

—

—Ok. I know. I know it's raining. We have large plate glass windows here. It's raining katzenjammers. It's raining like a cow pissing on a flat rock.

—

—There's nobody else here.

—

—Ok. I just gotta open this one box of Bantam and homeward I bound.

—

—Bantam. The publisher. One more box of books.

—

—I know. I don't know why it has to rain its hardest at rush hour. It's God thinning out the population.

—

—I know. Thanks, honey. I will. I will be careful.

*

—You really think it's just middle age, that I'm just having that cliché mid-life crisis?
—Why ask me?
—You're it, I'm afraid, buddy. This, *this*, is what friends do.
—I hadn't heard that.
—It's been in all the magazines.
—So.
—So, whaddya think? I'm getting tiresome, aren't I?
—Nah.
—You're swell. You know, you've always been swell.
—You too.

—How are things with you?

—Ok. Busy.

—Work?

—Yeah, that.

—Did you ever think we'd end up like this, both in retail in our forties? I mean, I sell books, it's all I know. I can't do anything else. And you, having your own art supply store—I mean I guess it seems right, you're an artist after all—but, *retail*. I don't know. It sounds so seventies. So mall-culture.

—Yeah. I think if I didn't work in retail I wouldn't actually mark the passage of time. That, you know, the holidays and stuff. What they mean is an increase in sales, in business, in how many people I see every day. What would Christmas be like if you didn't end up Christmas Eve tired as hell, having just peaked, so to speak? What does the guy at the insurance company, or the guy working the hub over at FedEx think of Christmas? How does he mark it?

—Well, FedEx. Christmas is probably busy—

—Yeah, yeah, bad example. You know what I mean.

—Yeah, I know. The difference between a one thousand-dollar day and a five thousand-dollar day is calendar oriented. You're right, that's how time passes. What needs we being come to sense but fumble in a greasy till.

—What?

—Yeats.

—Christ.

—Yeah, Yeats. He knew. Even back then. Didn't he work in a bookstore once?

—Hell, I wouldn't know. I barely know what you're talking about.

—Oh, bullshit. Don't do the subliterate act on me. Just because you make beauty out of color don't act like you haven't read a book.

—Right.

—So, middle age. You think it's really tough.

—I don't know, it's all right.

—Yeah, you're doing all right. So calm and serene, all your floundering behind you. How do you do it? You've been through the wringer just like me, second marriage, surprise pregnancies, surprise *false* pregnancies, the whole schmeer. How come you got so few scars? So little trouble coping?

—You're overestimating me.

—Really. Buddy, you seem so peaceful sometimes. I swear I think of you sometimes and wish I could draw on that inner strength, whatever you got. You're kind of a model, like it or not, an exemplum.

—Right. I'm really together. Christ, Jim, I haven't slept with my wife in months. How's that?

—I didn't know that.

—Well.

—That's rough.

—You said it.

—What's the problem?

—Just nonchalance, I think. I mean Ginger's great, you know. She's my best friend.

—God save us from best friends in bed.

—Ha. Well...

—At least I don't have that quandary. You know, Dorothea is still so hot. When I think about it—

—Spare me.

—Sorry.

—All right. But, there. Look at yourself.

—Yeah.

—You and your wife still get it on, what—

—Once a week, a little less—

—Damn. There you go.

—Yeah. That's pretty much something. That's pretty much lagniappe. Not that I don't miss that young thing—

—What, what else?

—You know, the abandon, the willingness to do it anywhere, car seats, front porches, in the living room with parents just around the corner and not even a closed door between you.

—Well. I'm not sure I have that kind of past to suffer.

—Don't bullshit me. I remember you and, what was her name, the cheerleader.

—Susan.

—Susan?

—They were all called Susan back then.

—Right. The stories you told me, I remember, you guys were pretty wild. There was something about a sleeping bag in the backyard and her father—

—Yeah, ha ha. That was wild. Susan—

—So.

—Ok.

—You miss that.

—Well, now, I mean since I've gone without—

—You haven't—

—No. Hell no. You know that'd kill Ginger.

—Yeah.

—You haven't—

—No.

—You don't sound as sure.

—Hey, I'm the one doing it steady, right?

—Never a proof against it.

—That's true.

—At any rate.

—Yeah. Hey, I ever tell you I was a twin once.

—What? What are you talking about?

—Before I was born. There was a second fetus but it didn't develop or something. Sometimes I think it still haunts me.

—Jesus.

—Yeah. I coulda been two. There was a twin but he didn't make it out of the ether.

—Just like Elvis.

—Yeah.

—You should have accomplished more.

*

—Hi. Need any help?

—Just looking.

—Help yourself.

—First time in. Just found out about you.

—Oh. Good. Make yourself at home. The whole store is a

mix of new and used. Some sections more new than used and some vice versa.

—How long has this been here, this store?

—1875.

—No kidding?

—No kidding.

—Well, I've always seen it and meant to come in.

—Well, help yourself, if I haven't already said that. Lemme know if you need anything. If you'd like to look at First Editions we keep them locked here in these cabinets in what we call our living room. I'll open any case you'd like.

—Thank you.

—Not at all.

—1875.

—Yep.

—Goodness.

—Course, I've only been here since about the turn of the century.

—Ha, ha.

—Our little joke.

—A good one.

*

—This party has caught fire.

—Outrageous, raging...

—It's an inferno.

—Not unlike Dante's.

—Ha.

—The one with the sweater, the one with all the earrings, Kris, Ed Hannigan's cousin from Hobbs, New Mexico, Hobbs for Christ's sake, the one with the legs dark lustrous revealed through skirt slit upon scissor stepping leg crossing etc., bulge of calf, the one with the Julie Christie lips, Helen D., a little too thin, but...

—Yes. All. All enchanting.

—You're married.

—Yes.

—Parties.

—Yes.

—This party.

—Yes.

—How to do it, how gracefully?

—Why go? Not to stay home.

—How make it natural; it's not natural. But the stimulus, still, getting outside yourself is important. For me, anyway.

—And me.

—Social animals. Public personae.

—None attractive, no public persona attractive.

—The herd instinct. Grazing.

—Man. Woman.

—The one with the hair, twin moles high on left cheek.

—Dated a woman like that once, twin moles. I called them magic, touched them at appropriate times, brought magic to them you might say. Beautiful woman, head turner, her ass, ah. And in bed.

God. She got a job at the hospital. Knew it was over. Started planning. Sure enough she fell in love with a male nurse.

—Never comfortable with that tag. Male nurse.

—Tanned like mahogany.

—I've known them.

—Ah.

—Yes.

—Knew a woman once had a single mole like a small island above her pubic hair. Like a signal that paradise was in sight, a beacon. When I think of that mole, now, I almost weep.

—Memory is dangerous.

—Memory is everything.

—Yes.

—Not enough to decide we are, we want also to signify.

—I like that.

—Can't live with them because we want to live within them.

—In a manner of speaking.

—And love. I've been in love, the ultimate aphrodisiac. Never better than when love is the impetus. Never more erotic, more fulfilling. Make it mean something, you know. The unquenchable urge, the bottomless well, like the Sorcerer's Apprentice. A fire that feeds itself.

—I've been there.

—In love. Makes everything else hollow, tepid, empty. Nothing like it. No love, life a shell.

—I had a girlfriend once named Angel, her real name. Names can be poems, incantations. I've paid attention to that, the list of names of exlovers, the poem it makes.

—Brooxie Short I had once. I had a Papatya once. Turkish,

I think she was.

—Open sesames. Anyway this girlfriend, this Angel, she was a joy, enrapturing, an envelope of tenderness and sensuality. She licked her fingers, stuck them full into her mouth—full-lipped she was, not unlike Julie Christie, not at all—and she'd take me into that wet paw, glide those slick fingers over my, um, member, if you see what I mean. Damn. Just thinking about it now...

—All gone, gone to mnemonics and cosmic dust.

—I think of her, I think of that. Unfair maybe. I remember so little else. Did we laugh, play Sorry? I don't know. That moisturizing trick is all that's left.

—Antonya used to tap my anus with one finger right before I'd come. Just tap tap tap until I let it go. I remember that and I remember her. We're reduced to that by age, by time's inexorable march. Remembered for our method, our one trick.

—At least that.

—One would like to think that one is the object of deepbedded passion.

—That some form of passion is still at work.

—Rare. Very rare.

—Mm.

—A list, you said. A list of names.

—Making a poem.

—How many do you imagine? A year I mean, at your peak?

—Tacky to relate to it that way.

—Yes, I know.

—Seven one year, less most other. I think seven might have been my best year. Seven new women, a few left over, with sadness and hopeless tremors from relationships past.

—Seven's good.

—Tacky. Bad taste.

—Yes.

—I used to send them Christmas cards. At the end of every year regardless of current status they'd get a Christmas card if I had exploded into them during the calendar year. If I had tasted their intimacy. Keeps the bitterness level low. Send those cards, message something like best wishes, hope this finds you well. A good gesture I think.

—Self-cleansing.

—Not exactly. But yes, unburdening.

—I guess Dorothea put the kibosh on that.

—Well, I voluntarily renounced. Best not to dwell on the romantic past once the marriage bed is made, once the nest is furnished. Expedient.

—Yes.

—Well, that year though…

—I love women.

—Yes.

—The smell, the differences, the catch-phrases. More mnemonics.

—Catch-phrases.

— *Buddyboy*, Veronica used to call me. *Who loves you baby?* was Linda's. *That's the ticket*, Lorrie used to say.

—Trish used to call me *Bucko*. Loved that. *Bucko*.

—Similar. Quite similar.

—Had a date once. In bed said, "Fuck me all night." Never forget her for those four words.

—Not unlike what I mean.

—Just saw her that once.

—Still.

—Hard these days. Hard to connect.

—Yes.

—Hard to strike that balance. Desire is important, passion, never underestimate it. But compatibility, friendship, trust. These things, at this time, seem irreducible.

—Trust, similar interests, communication. When to draw close, when to give space. When to express doubt, when to be strong, when weak. How close to get.

—All hard.

—Look around. Look at these women, this microcosm...

—Glad to be out of it.

—Yes, me too.

—Desirable. Calculations on a scale, desirability made art. Colorful clothing.

—Manipulation almost. No, too harsh.

—Push this button. This works. Madison Avenue. Vogue Magazine.

—But all delicious. All *there* nonetheless.

—No substance though. Light without heat.

—Well...

—Look at that blond, hair glowing, lit from within. Learns that. More tricks.

—Still.

—The one with the dimples, freckles and dimples.

—Cute. Nonintellectual.

—The one with the French braid, the jumpsuit.

—She's looking this way.

—Wayne Hineley's sister from Iowa.

—No, the roommate from Sweetbriar, Bob's ex-wife's college roommate.

—At any rate.

—Yes.

—She's smiling.

—Gorgeous, life-affirming.

—Makes you want to scream.

—I'm going to rip my own head off.

—This party.

—I'm burning, I'm a barn aflame. I'm in love...

—Yes. Yes, yes, yes.

*

—Didn't you just buy some feta?

—Jim, are you doing the refrigerator blindness thing again?

—Maybe. But, feta, do we have any?

—I honestly don't remember.

—How can you not remember feta?

—Jim.

—Alright.

—What do you want it for?

—Salad.

—We don't have any lettuce.

—Spinach salad.

—Jim, when have we ever had spinach?

—Ok.

—We're gonna eat in an hour anyway.

—Yeah. What's this? German mustard? When did we get German mustard? Why did we get German mustard?

—Sally gave it to us for Christmas.

—Which Christmas?

—You're exactly right. Throw it away.

—Be good on bratwurst.

—We don't have any bratwurst. As far as I know we have never had any bratwurst. We don't like bratwurst.

—Still. Be good with German mustard.

—Jim, are you even hungry?

—I don't know.

—You don't know if you're hungry? Jim, get out of the fridge. We'll eat soon. You want to go get Chinese?

—No.

—You don't want Chinese? You always want Chinese.

—I didn't say I didn't want Chinese. I said I didn't want to go get it.

—Right. You buy I fly.

—You got that from me.

—Yes.

—Can we get those little eggrolls, that ten pack?

—You told me those give you the runs.

—Yeah.

—But you want them anyway.

—They're good.

—Ok. What are you doing?

—What do you mean?

—Get out of the fridge.

—Right. Is this spoon fruit still good?

*

—I will

never again

kiss the

mole

which sits

like an island

above

your pubic

hair

and for this

I am

heartsick; for

this

I say

Confiteor.

*

—Who do you like here?

—You sound like Sports Center. Me? I like everybody. I like Coach K. I like that wiry forward on Stanford. I like the cheerleader third from right with the Asian haircut, though her hue is only California sun. She's as white as you and me.

—Who do you think is gonna win, to put it more precisely?

—Never bet against Duke. That's a credo to live by. Never bet against Coach K. Any year.

—Good credo.

—Thank you.

—Stanford's too white.

—Yeah. White means slow.

—White means clunky.

—White means mechanical.

—We better stop.

—Right.

—Duke still going full court?

—Press?

—Right.

—Yes. Duke always goes full court. Coach K. Sonofabitch.

—Right.

—End of the year, he'll be there. Doesn't matter what kind of year they've had, 25 and 2 or 19 and 10, he'll be there. Never bet against him.

—I don't.

—There she is. Cameraman loves her, too.

—She is fine. I think she is Asian.

—Naw.

—Look at her eyes.

—Just sloe-eyed, just sexy. She's as white as you or me.

—Actually I think I have some American Indian blood.

—Big deal, Jim. We all got Indian blood.

—Woo, woo.

—Right.

—Jeez, did you see that pass?

—Fuckin Duke.

—Passing fools.

—Passing fancy.

—Always with the point guard. History of great point guard.

—Tell me.

—Remember Hurley?

—God he was fun to watch.

—Had that car accident.

—Right.

—Woulda had a better pro career.

—He's still playing.

—Naw.

—Yes, he is. Canada or someplace.

—Canada. Can you believe the NBA is in Canada now?

—You're sounding kind of jingoistic.

—Jingleistic? You mean like an ad campaign?

—You know they're talking about Mexico.

—I know. NBA in Mexico. Won't be able to breathe. They'll have to pump oxygen into the arena.

—Right.

—Mexico.

—NBA's days are numbered. Had it all, went too far.

—They sold out years ago. Soon as they started having the Valvoline tip-off, the Wendy's half-time stats, the Preparation H dunk of the game.

—Yeah. The Pringles assist.

—Did you see that move?

—Not bad for a big white guy.

*

—Oh, the red slip.

—You love the red slip.

—Yes I do. I most decidedly do.

—Turn the light out and light a candle.

—Walk around a bit first. I love to watch that red slip move.

—Jim.

—Ok. Here. Now, come here.

—Mm.

—Oh it feels so good. So satiny.

—Silky.

—Whatever. Come closer my little silky.

—Mmm.

—You've got nothing on under this red slip.

—I know.

—I know you know.

—Mmm.

—You like that?

—Mm hm.

—Mm. I love your ass. Have I ever mentioned that?

—Once or twice.

—I love to feel that slip slide over it.

—Mmm.

—Oo, yeah. Rub yourself on my thigh.

—Mm hm.

—Oh.

—You're so hard.

—Yes.

—Mm.

—Mm, yes.

—Oh, take it out.

—You take it out for me.

—Mmm.

—Oh, God you do that nice.

—Mm, you feel nice.

—It's so hard.

—I know.

—I know you know.

—Mmm.

—Oh.

—

—

—Mm.

—Mmmmm.

*

—I took on that new clump of responsibilities and rewards, gratefully, and we did not have to work out in the yard in rough clothing, or paint the nursery, to feel part of the great wheel of things. We met, cohered, and save for an occasional whispering among the stars, our union was not so remarkable. Yet it is you I love and no one else and that is a splendid thing. So if I still cry quietly at night sitting in the same chair where you nursed our baby daughter not so long ago I am neither pitiful nor exceptional, one man feeling tethered to the wondrous, multivaried universe, humbled by it, made proud, alone and not, here at this loose end of life, the best one we could have created because we did it. And, because of you, I can soldier on, full of submissiveness and starlight.

*

—Hi. Can I help you?

—I've come to pick up my signed John Grissom.

—Um. Mr. *Grisham* hasn't been here yet. That's a week from Wednesday.

—I know. But my son's birthday is tomorrow. I wanted it to say, Happy Birthday, Timmy.

—Well. Mr. Grisham only signs his name I'm afraid.

—I was hoping something could be done. I was hoping you'd make an exception.

—Well, I can't. And, besides, you see, he won't be here until next week.

—Well, I thought you'd do me this favor seeing as how I buy my Grissom book here every year.

—Yes, ma'am. I'm sorry. We're bound by these rules. There's nothing I can do.

—Well, can I go ahead and get it today anyway. The one I ordered with just the signature?

—No ma'am. See, he hasn't been here yet. We haven't gotten *any* signed books yet.

—But I ordered an *advanced* copy.

—Yes ma'am.

—And I can't get that early.

—I'm sorry.

—Well, I don't see why you had me call ahead.

*

—So, you know I had my 25th high school reunion a couple of weekends ago.

—Yeah, how was that? I didn't even go to mine, didn't even consider it.

—Well, your feelings about such things are shared. Out of a class of 300 or so we had 67 people, and that's couples, so half of those, well, maybe less than half, were spouses, who, you know, stood around looking contemptuous.

—Yeah, that's what spouses are supposed to do.

—Yes. Well, it was all kind of depressing.

—Well, Jesus, Jim, why should you care? I mean, you of all people left that past far behind.

—You think so. Why, why me of all people?

—I don't know. You don't have much in common with those schnooks, do you? I mean, have any of them even read a book since high school?

—Right. I know. But they're important to me just the same. I don't know. Whatever I've become, I like to believe there's a thread linking me to my past, to these people who were so crucial to me at a major point in my life, who helped form me, I guess. For better or worse.

—Do you ever talk to any of these guys, I mean between reunions?

—No.

—So.

—Look, I know. But there's still this connection, you know.

I can't explain it but high school was such a formative time for me. Maybe the last time I was fully confident, fully myself. Maybe it's been downhill ever since.

—Now that's a depressing thought.

—Do you not ever feel that way?

—You mean like I was at my best in 1973 when I was eighteen. I know that's the male sexual peak but lemme tell you I was one geeky high schooler and now, with my wife and all, having my own place, no Jim, this is the pinnacle.

—I know, I know, me too. I mean physically, *in the world*, yes. But in my leaky head I think I was better then. I mean it's sort of not fair to Dorothea, she's not getting the best of me.

—I don't know, Jim. You know, I knew you back then. You were charming and all, Jesus look at all the girls you had. But I think I like you better now.

—I don't.

—Really?

—No, I don't know. I am better now. Smarter, more capable in some ways. Able to take on the big guys, that old joker Joyce, Gaddis, Gass. Am I nicer, calmer, more outgoing? I don't think so.

—So you're nostalgic for your high school days and the reunion was a bummer and it woke you up to the disparity.

—Sort of. I mean, I think this middle age thing, hitting my forties, it's become such a period of introspection for me. I guess I've always been too self-oriented, so full of awareness that I can't even walk across a room without thinking *I'm walking across the room*, but anyway, now, I've been mulling over things, everything. I mean, I've been at my whole past with a fine toothed comb, thinking a lot about my childhood, my parents, the legacy my mother has left me—this sort of chemical neuron misfiring I blame on her, you know my inherited nervousness. Anyway this attempting to figure it all out, I think it has something to do with the kids, I wanna pass on a positive image for them, don't want to make the mistakes my folks made, so I have to concentrate and recognize all the signposts along my highway and decipher all the symbols and filter it through my consciousness and have it for them, you know. Have the answer.

—Meanwhile your kids grow up and it slips away, I mean while you're doing all this cogitating.

—Yes, that hurts, but yes. But, see, I've always been trapped in my own head.

—I know, Jim. I know, me too.

—Yeah. But now for some reason I feel like I've got to figure it all out. Or, it's not that clearly delineated, this is just me trying to figure out what I'm doing.

—Trying to figure out the figuring out.

—Damn. It's a labyrinth, isn't it?

—Let's hope the Minotaur is only in our own heads, right?

—Ha, yeah.

—So the reunion. Did you see Laurie?

—You have been paying attention.

—Don't want to talk about it?

—No no. It's just, you know, Dorothea didn't go with me and there I was, all alone and, let's be honest, thinking about my profligate younger self and hoping to see Laurie and hoping she's thinking about that kind of thing—it's what reunions are all about, isn't it?

—And she was there and it was disappointing.

—No, I mean, yes she was there. And yes it was disappointing but not for the reason you mean.

—She's fat and dull.

—Ha, no. She looked great.

—Really?

—Yeah, two kids and she looked great. Still got the waist of a schoolgirl and that magnificent butt, those runner's thighs.

—But what?

—Nothing. She looked great, she was happy to see me.

—That is horrible.

—Ok, ok. She came right over to me. Evening about half gone when she arrived and I saw her come in and she chatted with Iris and them for a few minutes and turned her head to me and—big smile—made a beeline. For me. It was great to see her. All the bad stuff slipped away and we hugged and smiled a lot and asked about each other's kids. She lives in Atlanta now and her husband, of course, didn't come with her, stayed there with the kids. And we stood there grinning like a couple of ninnies and I think some folks were looking at us with these sort of knowing smirks and it was high school all over again.

—But the disappointment was that was all and you came home and life resumed. You stepped outside it for a brief shining moment and then reality returned.

—You're so wise and knowing. No, that wasn't quite it.

—Ok.

—They had this kind of hallway at this ballroom, some kind of like access thing and it was dark and shadowy and somehow Laurie and I ended up there, chatting amiably the whole time and I knew, I just knew, she was thinking what I was thinking, even if it was just, what would it be like to make it again after all this time.

—Wait, didn't you see her at the 20th?

—No, it had been fifteen years. She didn't come to the 20th, it had been since the tenth. And then, there was still all this poison in the air between us, we barely spoke. Ridiculous, but after ten years we hadn't shaken the bad feelings. It took 25 years, I guess.

—I'm on the edge of my seat here. You didn't have her in the access thing?

—No, life isn't like that, Mark. But we kissed long and deep and her fat warm tongue was in my mouth and, I swear, 25 years melted away. Just like that, as if her precious tongue were a madeleine.

—Damn.

—Yeah.

—Nothing else though, no wandering hands.

—Well, I mean, you know, that butt. I think I did hold it while we kissed.

—Well then.

—Yeah. And at the end of the evening we hugged and swapped pleasantries and vowed to keep in touch and I drove home feeling guilty and thrilled and kind of sick and I knew that I wouldn't talk to her again for another five years.

—That's reunions. That's reunions in a nutshell. I think you just hit the essence of reunions, the distilled essence.

—Right.

—So, while all this sentimental re-coupling was going on, did you have time for anyone else? Did you even talk to anyone else?

—Yeah, I did. But, like I said, there weren't that many people there. Mostly it was folks I run into occasionally anyway. Well, that's not entirely true. It was actually great to talk to Glen and Jimmy again, two guys I really palled around with back then whom I haven't talked to much since. Again, every time we see each other there's the vow to call, to keep in touch.

—But, really you don't have much in common with these guys.

—I don't know. The gang I hung with in high school, I mean, looking back, there was a real sharpness there, a knowing sort of wisdom. I think we all kept each other honest, didn't allow any bullshit to exist among us, and I think, in a sense, this is what I meant by that cord which stretches back to that time. Some of these guys, Steve Waterman, Freddie, Billy Samonides, the Lederer girls, Amy What-was-her name. This was a pretty sharp bunch. And we had this thing between us, among us, whenever anyone made a comment that was a little phony, a little high-faluting, we had this tag-line. I mean, say something the least bit artificial and someone would pipe up with, "Are we acting?" With just that kind of lilt to it, *Are we acting?* And, I think I owe a lot to this kind of friendly exactitude, this call for self inspection, this kind of honesty. We didn't allow any counterfeit crap to pass unexamined.

—Jeez, I don't know. I don't think I would have stood up well under that kind of scrutiny.

—Well, I don't want to oversell it. It's just something I've been thinking about. Oh, and you should have seen what Waterman wrote in my annual. See, Steve graduated in '72 and his parting shot to me, to see me off into my senior year, was this screed about what a disappointment I was to him. I mean he used my annual to read me the riot act. It was full of venom, this submerged venom which somehow sprung forth onto the glossy page of my yearbook.

—What did he say?

—You can guess. I have all this potential, according to him, all this talent, and instead of applying myself I was content to chase, and this phrase has stuck with me, "every big-titted piece of ass in the school." It was like if he had all my gifts, blah blah blah, what he would be doing, and keep in mind this is a guy who was smarter than me, funnier than me, I was really kind of in awe of him, kind of constantly surprised he was my friend, constantly thinking he was gonna see through me and call me on the carpet. Well, I guess he finally did.

—Jesus. And this kind of honesty you really think you needed, you think this was positive?

—No, I don't know. I mean I was really hurt by it and it stayed with me and its validity I never questioned. I mean, he was right, and I needed to hear it and today I could still take it to heart. Though, did I change, for better or worse? I don't know.

—It sounds more to me like he was a little jealous.

—Oh, sure. I mean, all these intellectual guys want to picture themselves as above the hungers of the flesh, as if they have a higher calling to a life of the mind and women are a secondary consideration.

—Steve didn't get much tail in high school.

—Right.

—And you did.

—Well. But it doesn't mean he wasn't right.

—And you were friends with this guy later?

—Not really. But not, I think because of this diatribe. We just sort of drifted apart. I mean, he apologized later, said he'd been up all night on speed cramming for exams. But I think he was really glad he'd said it all, even if a little embarrassed that he'd made a permanent record of it in my annual.

—And your overall feeling left over from this reunion evening was, what? Wistful longing? Sexual longing?

—Little of both maybe.

—Thinking about Laurie?

—No, well, yeah. I mean, of course. Fantasizing a little, guiltily. You know, ha, that butt, I mean, she might age around it but that butt is staying pristine, young and ripe like a peach.

—You sure you didn't do more than hold it?

—I didn't. You know, Dorothea and the kids and my peaceful nest of a life. I can't, wouldn't want to do anything to upset that.

—Uh huh.

—That's maturity, right? I mean Steve would be proud of me, right? Really, if I wanted to stray—I mean more than a tongue kiss in an access way, more than a squeeze of a still firm buttock—all I have to do is think about how much I'm risking. I mean, it's a wonderful life, right?

—Are we acting?

*

—Hello?

—

—Hi, ma.

—

—No, they got there alright. Yeah, everyone's fine, kids are great.

—

—Still a little runny nose, I think, but you know, Katey, full of herself and loves an audience. I think the in-laws will spoil her sufficiently.

—

—Yeah, I'm fine. Lonely, sure.

—

—Because I'm alone, why do you think? I'm all alone in this uninsulated house, wandering like a ghost between rooms, dreaming of the life which once blossomed here.

—

—I was just joking, ma. I mean the flowery part. I really am lonely, just, you know, missing the wife and kids.

—

—I will. Gonna make myself some dinner here, watch a movie.

—

—Chicken livers.

—

—Yeah, well, I gotta fix em when Dorothea's not here. She can't stand the sight of them.

—

—You know my wacky wife, ma. She only has ten foods she eats. I could be a better cook, well, maybe a little better, if I had the support to follow my inspiration and experiment with new dishes. But, if it's not pasta and not shrimp Dorothea's gonna only politely say it's good while she chokes it down with some ice tea.

—

—You know why I didn't go.

—

—I don't travel well these days, ma. I know, it's not fair to the in-laws, not fair to Dorothea. But, self-preservation takes over.

—

—You know, nausea, panic. I'm a fun match. I think Dorothea is real happy with her choice of mates, really thinks she got a catch.

—

—I'm just joking, sort of. Dorothea and I are fine.

—

—Yes, she loves me. Yes, I know.

—

—Ok, ma.

—

—I will, ma. You too.

—

—Bye, ma.

*

—And everyone's okay in Itta Bena?
—Oh, sure. Manny was intent on passing another kidney stone while we were there but other than that unpleasantness things were swell. Abundance and relish.
—And your grandmother's cornbread dressing.
—Yes. She's sent some back with me.
—Sainted woman. Kids good?

—As always. Katey is still spilling over with dramatic flair and histrionics. She has such an audience there. And Conrad, of course, I didn't see him the whole time. I think he and Martin stayed in Martin's room the entire trip, new video game, you know? Space stoners, or Crypt cheaters, or something. It was a big hit.

—Well, good. Good to have you back.

—Mm, good to be back. What's that smell?

—Um, frying grease, I think. It seems to be lingering. That was night before last and it's like the thing that wouldn't die. I lit that vanilla candle in here but the grease odor seems to be more powerful, a living entity. We are haunted by the shades of livers past.

—What did you fry? You never fry.

—I never fry when you're here because you don't like fried foods. And, now I have a new reason not to fry. The stench sticks around.

—So, what did you fry?

—You don't want to hear it.

—Ok.

—Chicken livers.

—Oh, literally livers. You're right. I didn't want to hear it.

*

—Pops, you want to see my new drawings.

—You know I do.

—Martin did the one on the right.

—These are marvelous. You've got the gift of perfect lines, I've told you that.

—Thanks, Pops.

—You know I love it when you call me Pops.

—Ok, Pops.

—What, what is this? An alien?

—That's a burning bush.

—Like in Moses.

—What?

—Never mind. So this guy is talking to a burning bush.

—That's the alien. He's set the bush on fire because this guy was hiding behind it.

—Uh huh. And what's this guy doing?

—Martin drew that one. He's throwing up blood.

—Nice.

—Martin drew that one.

—That's ok. No prohibition on subject matter from me. I'll not limit your artistic leeway.

—You're funny, Pops.

—Why is that funny?

—Did Mom tell you about the new game I got?

—Space cheaters?

—What? Galaxy Corps.

—Corpse?

—C-o-r-p-s.

—That's "core."

—Oh.

—That's ok. It's a good game?

—Yeah. You wanna watch me play it?

—Oh, Connie, you know it's not fun to watch someone else play.

—Martin and I watch each other.

—Well, you have a higher tolerance for non-interaction.

—Huh?

—Nothing. You can show me how to play it sometime.

—You wanna come play it?

—Not right now.

*

—Read a book?

—Of course, Princess.

—In the snack chair.

—Yes. You go get me one.

—Ok. I'll go get one.

—Pick a short one. Daddy's tired.

—This one.

—*Arthur's Halloween.* Honey, that's a long one. And Halloween's long gone.

—But we'll have another one.

—Yes, next year.

—And we'll trick or treat and get candy.

—Yes.

—And I'll get candy.

—Yes. And you'll be—

—And I'll be Tinky Winky.

—Right. You might wanna be someone new next year.

—No, I'll be Tinky Winky.

—Ok.

—And Connie will be an alien.

—Yes, just like this year.

—And Connie will be an alien.

—Yes.

*

—Mm, baby.

—The red slip *and* a porno movie. Isn't this over-stimulation? Aren't we afraid of peaking too early?

—Naw. Snuggle up against me here.

—Is this the new movie?

—Yes.

—You bought this one? You really shouldn't buy them, you know. What if the kids find them?

—They won't. This was so cheap it didn't seem worth paying to rent one. They sell off the old stock and perverts like us benefit.

—Uh huh.

—I'm betting this doctor and this patient are about to violate the honorable code of the medical profession.

—Safe bet. At least the woman is good looking in this one.

—She is, isn't she? What about the doctor? Is he a turn on?

—The men rarely are in these things. Until, of course, he unsheafs his sword.

—Yeah, I guess they're hired for pretty much one physical attribute.

—Looks like they're fixing to get to that attribute.

—Yep. There goes his Hippocratic oath.

—And her top.

—Nice tits.

—Mm hm.

—Oh my. She's lying on his desk. And, yep, here comes his physical attribute.

—Whoa.

—Uh huh.

—Now there's a nice trick.

—I'll say. You wanna try it?

—I'd throw my back out. Look at the size of that thing.

—It's a pretty one. Kind of puts mine in the shade, he said in a moment of self-doubt.

—Hey, yours is just right.

—Feel it right now. It's—mm—

—Yes, it is.

—Look what they do now.

—They're making the best of that desk, I'll say.

—Yes, and, mm, rub up against me while we watch this.

—Mm hmm. Like that?

—Uh huh.

—Now they're getting down to business. I like it when they get past the oral stuff and into the down and dirty.

—I know you do.

—Slip those off now.

—Oh. Mm.

—This is working for me. Wanna turn the movie off now?

—Not just yet. I like to watch them while you stroke me.

—Mmm. I'm getting kind of horny here.

—Kind of. Just wait a minute. I'm betting—mm—they get to the rear entry position.

—Okey dokey. Mmmm.

—And there it is, our favorite.

—Mmm hmm.

—Oh my. Lookit—mm—oh my—

—Yes, dear—mmm—

—Just—mm—oh—

—Don't you—mm—come just yet—

—Ok. Turn it—mmm—off——

—C'mere——

*

—And then we did it like dirty children.

—Wait a minute. You're telling me you watch porno movies to gear you up?

—Yes, don't you?

—Well, gosh. You know I've never considered it. I'm not sure Ginger would—

—Gosh? Ginger's no prude.

—No. Decidedly not.

—Well, then.

—I might just suggest it. Where do you, you know, get them?

—The, uh, video store.

—They've got the good ones.

—At the store out east, not the Midtown one.

—I'll be damned. Porno.

—Welcome to the real world, Mark buddy. Tell me something. That woman who works with you, Katya?

—What about her?

—I saw her the other day.

—You did, where?

—Coming out of the video store.

—Jesus, when you were getting pornography?

—No, actually. Don't hyperventilate. I was renting, let's see, I think it was *The Postman*.

—The foreign film.

—No, the Kevin Costner thing.

—Oh, right. That's supposed to be awful.

—I know. It was better than its reputation. Not bad really. A little too long but what film in these indulgent days is not?

—Isn't Mary Steenburgen in that?

—No.

—Yes, she is. No, wait, not Mary Steenburgen, the woman from that TV show.

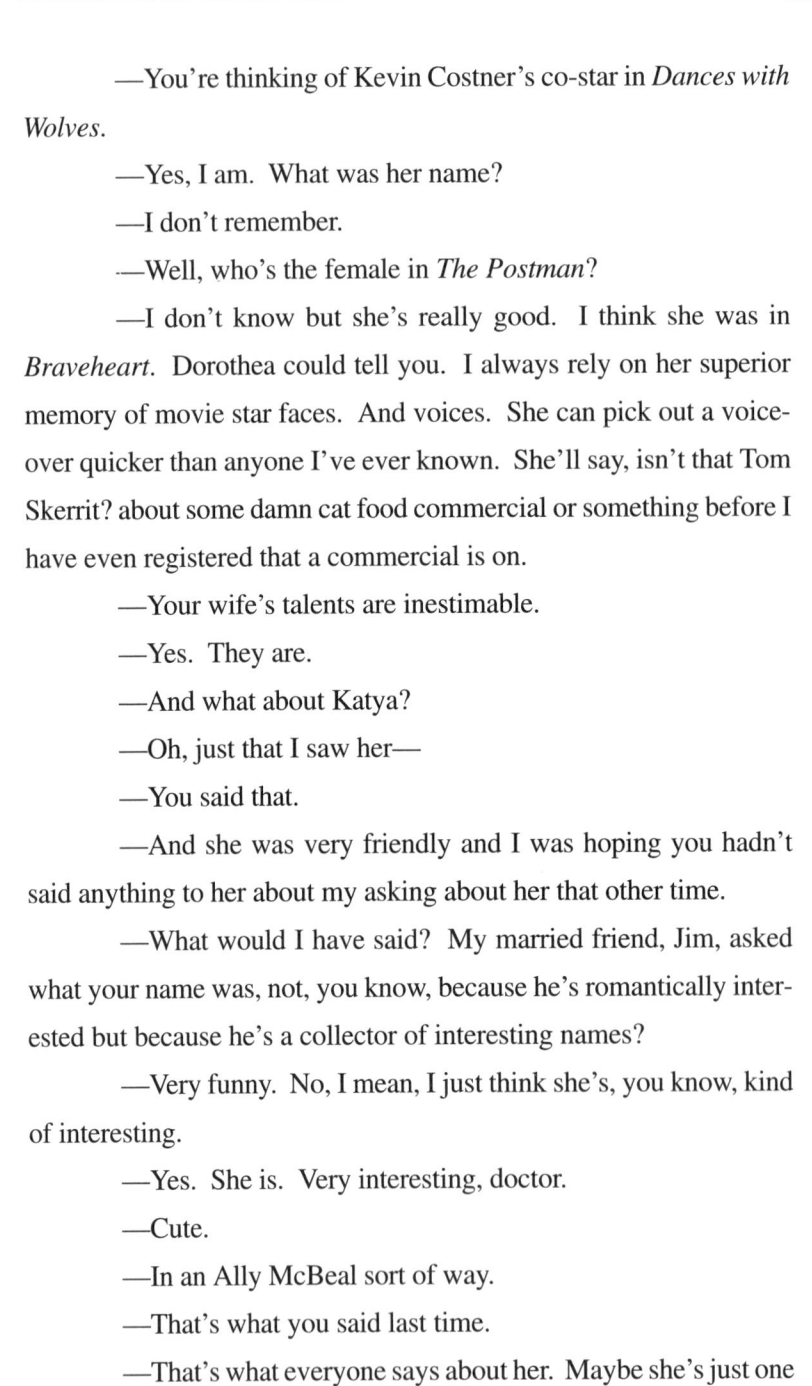

—You're thinking of Kevin Costner's co-star in *Dances with Wolves*.

—Yes, I am. What was her name?

—I don't remember.

—Well, who's the female in *The Postman*?

—I don't know but she's really good. I think she was in *Braveheart*. Dorothea could tell you. I always rely on her superior memory of movie star faces. And voices. She can pick out a voice-over quicker than anyone I've ever known. She'll say, isn't that Tom Skerrit? about some damn cat food commercial or something before I have even registered that a commercial is on.

—Your wife's talents are inestimable.

—Yes. They are.

—And what about Katya?

—Oh, just that I saw her—

—You said that.

—And she was very friendly and I was hoping you hadn't said anything to her about my asking about her that other time.

—What would I have said? My married friend, Jim, asked what your name was, not, you know, because he's romantically interested but because he's a collector of interesting names?

—Very funny. No, I mean, I just think she's, you know, kind of interesting.

—Yes. She is. Very interesting, doctor.

—Cute.

—In an Ally McBeal sort of way.

—That's what you said last time.

—That's what everyone says about her. Maybe she's just one of those quasi-attractive women who look like whoever is currently hot in the public consciousness.

—Maybe so. But she's a little cuter than quasi.

—Semi-quasi.

—Ok. She's got a nice butt.

—Ok, Mr. Smooth. You've noticed more than how interesting she is.

—I am but flesh and blood. Am I not a man?

—A happily married man.

—Yes, that's true. Though no proof against temptation I've found. One can be simultaneously very much in love with one's wife and still want to sleep with another woman. It's a tough realization, but there it is. As real as it gets. That's about as honest as I can be, human-beingwise.

—And you want to sleep with Katya?

—No, no. Don't infer. I'm just making conversation. Conversation between two old friends, who are very sympathetic and discreet.

—Right, I know.

—Like you're not tempted.

—I know.

—Whom?

—Forget it. This is getting out of hand.

—It's just talk. One thing no one can ever take from you is the fantasy life in your head. This is what we're talking about.

—Halle Berry.

—That's not realistic.

—I thought we were talking fantasy.

—Fantasy has to be grounded. That's—science fiction—

—Oh, thanks. Your fantasy love life you dignify, mine gets

denigrated.

—Sorry. Halle Berry, now that you mention it—

—She's mine.

—Ha ha. Anyone else?

—Well, we did have this receptionist once. College girl, horn rim glasses. Kind of homely really. But something about her just set the bugs loose in me. The way she bumped around in her dress just moving across the room, the way her legs seemed to be bunched muscles, her thighs—

—Now we're talking.

—Anyway. Even talk can be dangerous. Ginger's it for me.

—Right. And Dorothea for me.

—Ok.

—Forget I asked about Katya. Just ran into her and thought I'd mention it. Nothing else implied.

—Ok. What ever happened to Mary Steenburgen?

*

—Hello, Dodo.

—Jim, you know I hate those kinds of diminutives. Especially that one.

—Except in bed, where sobriquets come out sexy and irresistible.

—No, I hate them even in bed, though often there I am defenseless.

—Lost to the moment, you are.

—Something like that. Don't call me Dodo.

—Right.

—You're grinning like a potentate.

—Am I?

—Why so pleased with yourself? What are you watching?

—Oh, nothing now.

—Mr. Literal. What *were* you watching?

—Game.

—Basketball game.

—Right.

—And your team won.

—Um, right.

—Your beloved Tigers won. And you sit there grinning like it's some personal accomplishment.

—Well.

—You're a sweet man, Jim. But you're a little pitiful.

—Don't you want me happy? Doesn't it warm your very cockles to see a smile on your beloved's beloved face?

—Leave my cockles out of it. Of course, I'm happy you're happy, Sweet. But it's a fragile thing, isn't it?

—None the less a cause for observance.

—Stop talking so whimsically. I mean, if your Tigers—and I don't accept that possessive pronoun, though I bow to its general use—if your Tigers had lost, you'd be moping around here like—like—

—Johnny Parker.

—Ha. I don't know what like. You know what I mean.

—Like a mouse without cheese?

—Ok.

—Like an angel for a good man's sins?

—Stop, Jim.

—Like a paper bag full of sour milk?

—I'm leaving.

—I love you.

—I know you do.

—You love me, too. Dodo.

*

—The phone rings at midnight and I stumble to answer. It could be anyone: my mother with bad news, my ex-wife, telephone solicitors with their pathetic babble, the president unfamiliar with time zones promising me a position in our new government.

This time, though, it is a foul-mouthed drunk, calling me by name, slurring epithets. I hang up, she calls right back. I have to disconnect myself from the world. "Again?" my wife asks, when I return to bed. Yes, I tell her, disgusted, not that I'm above reproach, disdain, abuse. I lie awake and imagine a different call, a night of despair. Or, I imagine the world at rest, except for a few sad souls, mouths pinched around receivers, denied sleep, cursed to dial that number over and over.

*

—Hello.

—

—Hi, Ma.

—

—Yes, of course they're back, Ma. It's been a week.

—

—I know. I know what you meant.

—

—

—Yes. I'm sorry.

—

—Tomorrow.

—

—Tomorrow, Ma. We have to be out that way anyway. Connie wants some paintball supplies from that place on 64 near your house.

—

—Paintball. I can't explain it. It's a game.

—

—No, we'll come out there. I don't want you driving in.

—

—I know. But Dad's eyes, you know.

—

—I know.

—

—Ok, Ma.

—

—Ok.

*

—You know my mother's a hoot.

—So you always say. Is this our theme tonight? You know I love your mother. She's about as sweet as they come.

—I know you do. I do too, of course. But, I mean, she's nuts. You know, just a little.

—They all are. That whole generation of mothers. Something about the war or the depression, which they took literally. Something about birthing babies and sex before it all became living room discourse. How would you like to have had to have sex in the 1930s or 40s or even 50s? Jesus, they couldn't talk about it, they couldn't act like they wanted it. It took its toll is my theory.

—I don't know. I think that's a form of romanticizing the past. I think they were just as highly charged sexually as we are, maybe more so. Look what they're discovering about the Victorian era. All that repression led to Jane Austen and George Eliot but also the dear Marquis. I have a feeling the Marquis' vision has always been as prevalent as prim Ms. Austen's. Sexuality is like the lava under the earth. It's always there and it's always ready to bubble out.

—Another one of your perverse sexual metaphors. What was that other one? Something about bandages, or cotton?

—You're referring, of course, to my groundbreaking Q-tip Theory of Sexuality.

—Right. How does that go?

—You embarrass me but I'll elucidate one more time. It all has to do with God as C student, the God we got as opposed to the Possibility of God. Ours has very good intentions, very good ideas, really, but little in the way of talent of execution. I take that back: he's a-one at *execution*. But, for fixing life up all spiffy and convenient and comfortable, he's a little lacking.

—You'll burn in hell for this.

—Quite probably hell is just as inefficient and I will be only mildly singed, perhaps sunburned.

—Ha ha.

—Anyway, you know the ideas are all in place but they don't quite function as productively as intended. I mean, when we get hot we sweat. A good idea but it doesn't cool us down as well as it should. And, conversely, when we are cold we shiver but it doesn't warm us up.

—Get to the sex part.

—Patience, my raggle-taggle protégé. Now, we come to sexuality. A wonderful idea. A life-affirming, robust celebration of the very essence of humanness, a revelry of the very flesh we walk around in. But, whoops, it's also dangerous. There are diseases, disgusting diseases which rot away the very apparati with which we enjoy our pleasures. And now AIDS—too depressing really to even include in one's theorizing. Not to mention unwanted pregnancy, children where we only wanted to have it off a little. And, in this way, it is like the Q-tip. Everyone knows sticking a q-tip too deeply in your ear can be injurious, can puncture the drum or whatever and hurt like hell and possibly cause permanent damage to our hearing. And yet, and yet—it *feels so good.* My point being, what kind of God makes it feel so good if it's so hazardous? A C-student God.

—You're a trip.

—Makes sense, though.

—Not everything that makes sense is worth proclaiming.

—You got me there. Ha.

—What were we talking about?

—My mother.

—Right.

—Um. So she calls me up to ask if Dorothea is back yet?

—So?

—It's been a week. So what she's really doing is asking me if my life is back in order. If, now that spouse and children are back in place, am I not happier, more secure.

—Jim, really. Give her a break. You're reading much too much into that.

—You think so? You don't know my mother like I do.

—Well, explicitly not.

—I know. I am hard on her. It's just this re-thinking my life I've been doing. She has become the culprit.

—You know everyone's looking for the roots of their psychoses. I fear it's a way of not accepting personal responsibility.

—Thanks a lot.

—You know what I mean. Not just you. Everyone. But I don't want you to blame some wild psychological theories if there's something right in front of you which can help you more.

—You sound like a guru. What are you talking about?

—I don't know. Just talking.

—You didn't have anything specific in mind? Something which I'm missing, something to help me?

—No, I really didn't.

—Well, my mother, though. You know, I've told you about Johnny Parker.

—Remind me.

—Well, all my life my mother told my brother and me, anytime we were screwing up in her estimation, anytime we didn't look quite right, our clothes, or, in the 60s, our hair. Her comment was always, "You're not going out like that. You look like Johnny Parker."

—And, Johnny Parker was who, like the neighborhood ragman, or something?

—No, no. Nothing so easily digested, nothing so plain. Years later we're sitting around talking with my mother's sisters, you know all my crazy Canadian aunts, no, wait it was at my parent's 50th anniversary party and I made that speech about my growing up that got such big laughs. Well, the biggest laugh I got was when I made mention of my mother's aphorism, when I mentioned the name Johnny Parker. It got, what you might call, a better reaction than I had anticipated. And, afterwards, one of my aunts, still wiping tears of laughter from her eyes, came up and said, you know who Johnny Parker was, don't you, Jim? I allowed as to how we just sort of took it as a queer Canuck expression, something like, well I swannee, or wouldn't that rot your socks. No, no, she says. Johnny Parker was the retarded boy in their neighborhood when they were growing up.

—Oh, Jesus.

—Yes.

—Well, that is pretty bad.

—Ok then.

—I guess that is pretty small minded.

—Hey, don't go too far. That's my mother you're talking about.

*

—*Arsenic and Old Lace.*

—*His Girl Friday.*

—*North by Northwest.*

—Good one. Obvious but a good one. *None but the Lonely Heart.*

—What's that?

—Oh, it's great. Gritty, supposedly not one of Cary's personal favorites, hits too close to the bone or something. He plays a bit of a dirty dog.

—*Bishop's Wife.*

—*Topper.*

—Ha. Ha ha. Hadn't thought about that one in a while.

—Let's do someone else.

—*Philadelphia Story.*

—You know, I don't think *Philadelphia Story* is that great. I know everyone loves it, great cast and all, but I never thought it was great. I always preferred *Holiday*.

—*Holiday*.

—Good one. Let's do someone else.

—Ok. Favorite, um—

—Ian Holm films.

—C'mon. Favorite—

—Bela Lugosi.

—*Dracula*. End of story.

—You're right.

—Peter Lorre.

—Tough one. *Casablanca*—

—*M*.

—Oo, yeah. *Maltese Falcon*.

—*Arsenic and Old Lace*.

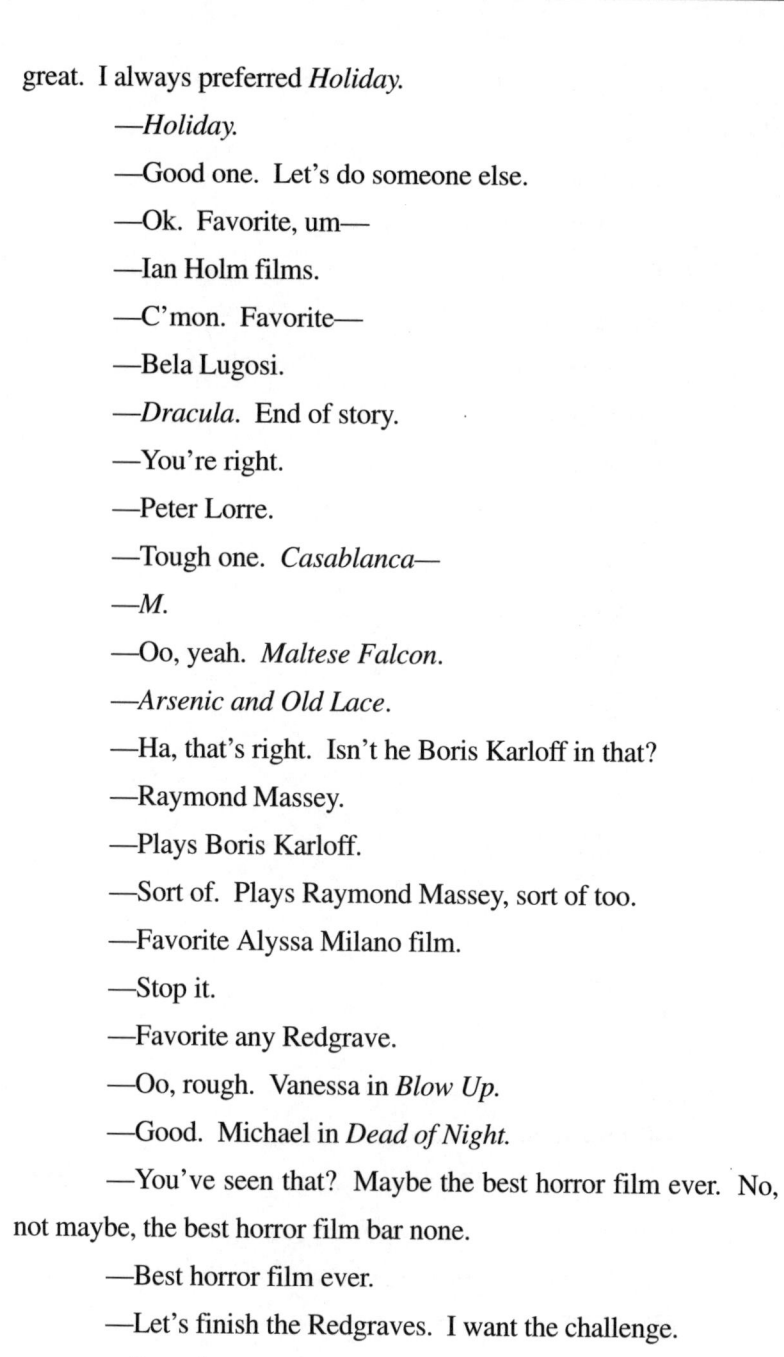

—Ha, that's right. Isn't he Boris Karloff in that?

—Raymond Massey.

—Plays Boris Karloff.

—Sort of. Plays Raymond Massey, sort of too.

—Favorite Alyssa Milano film.

—Stop it.

—Favorite any Redgrave.

—Oo, rough. Vanessa in *Blow Up*.

—Good. Michael in *Dead of Night*.

—You've seen that? Maybe the best horror film ever. No, not maybe, the best horror film bar none.

—Best horror film ever.

—Let's finish the Redgraves. I want the challenge.

—Lynn in—

—*Georgy Girl*, yeah, yeah.

—I was gonna say *Everything You Always Wanted to Know About Sex*.

—She was in that?

—First vignette. With the court jester.

—Right.

—Vanessa in *Julia*.

—Eh, too stuffy. Michael in *The Browning Version*.

—Vanessa in *The Devils*.

—Oo, kinky.

—Favorite Heather Graham film.

—Anything.

—I did that just for you.

—I love her. I love Heather Graham.

—I know.

*

—We gotta get another bathroom.

—I'll run right down and pick one up.

—No, really, Jim. I hate this in the morning getting four people ready. It's only gonna get worse as Katey gets older.

—I don't mind you coming in while I'm bathing. Gives us time to talk.

—What's that smell?

—New dandruff shampoo. I got it at Wild Oats.

—Does it work?

—Not yet. But this is the first time I've used it. I love the smell of pine tar in the morning. It smells like...

—Telephone poles.

—Exactly.

*

—What's new?

—Tell me again how you rented the porno film?

—You talked to Ginger about it?

—No, I thought I'd surprise her.

—Bad idea.

—You think so?

—Yeah. Women are a little weird about, you know, the sex thing. In my experience. Best not to spring new things on them.

—You're probably right.

—Like the last time I rented one I drove out to the east store and picked through their fascinating selection. By the way it's an art picking the right one. You can kinda judge by the picture of the woman on the box, I mean if she's good looking or hard looking or whatever, but sometimes the woman on the box is not even in the film.

—Interesting. You've made quite a study of this.

—Yeah. On the back, now that's a little better, though more times than not, the store has magic markered through the sexual parts.

But still you can get a good idea. Normally the back of the box has all these stills from the film, actual scenes from the movie, so depending on your proclivity, you can see kinda what turns you on, be it dogstyle, oral, large breasts, whatever. Still you'll get some of these home and they are just not good turnons, not quite up to snuff. I don't know exactly what the difference is; I'm still studying it.

—Thanks from all of us.

—Right. Sometimes you get some of these dogs home and they're actually anerotic, something about the people in them, the lack of style, the subtlety of the foreplay.

—Subtlety? Really?

—Well, in a sense. Not subtlety like Bergman, but, you know, some do it better than others.

—Ok.

—Anyway what I was saying, I went into the store and picked out what I thought was a good one and took it, rather sheepishly, up to the desk. I mean I'm still a little embarrassed by the process, though the clerks at this store have mastered the poker face. They put that dungy commodity in the sack and take your money just as if you were taking home the latest Ron Howard. Professionalism, I appreciate it. Anyway, there behind the desk, was the boyfriend of a woman I used to work with. Just one of those vague acquaintances, maybe he'll recognize me, maybe not. Well, of course, he does. And I laugh, a little embarrassed, and say something like, Don't tell Marge, that's the girlfriend, ha ha, just between us men, etc. I mean, I thought it was pretty funny.

—And it is.

—Yes. But I get home to the wife and tell her this comical anecdote and she's grim. I mean she's crestfallen.

—Positively crestfallen.

—Yes. And, she's all, this is gonna be all over midtown, all our friends will know, and on and on. And I say, you know, so?

—Right.

—And, anyway, that's women. Figure that out.

—And did you then use the aforementioned film to aid you in your intimate engagement?

—Oh, sure. So it wasn't a total turnoff, I guess. Dorothea, you might say, rose to the occasion all the same.

—Good. And was the film a good one?

—Oh boy.

—What was it called? Maybe we'll start with that one.

—I have no idea.

—You don't remember?

—I'm not sure I ever even registered it. The titles mean nothing. Frequently they are plays on the titles of currently popular movies, *Hannah Does Her Sisters, Bravehardon, Sperm of Endearment, Fill Monty, Howard's Rear-end*, crap like that. Really lame word play, but then you're not dealing with Paddy Chayevsky here.

—Ha, right.

—Anyway, Mark. I highly recommend you talk to Ginger first.

—I bow to your larger experience.

—Right.

—Whaddya wanna talk about now?

—You mean after sex. Cigarettes?

—Sure. Can you even fathom that you used to smoke?

—Yeah. I know. I still miss it though.

—Really? I don't get that? Never having smoked, never

having been even tempted to smoke, I don't get the desire to.

—When you've loved and lost...

—Right. Hey, have you noticed that people don't even look up anymore when a siren goes by? I mean, when we were kids a siren was a big deal. It sort of struck terror in our hearts, it meant something was seriously wrong. If a police car or ambulance went down our street with its siren blaring we were all given pause. Is Mrs. Murphy sick? Is Old Man Hickman dead at last? Did the fireman who lived two doors down come home drunk again, flatten the hydrant next to his driveway, and proceed to beat his wife, again? We'd stand there with our football tucked under our arm—our collective arm—and stare after the vehicle as if it had offended our comfort, broken the stillness which enveloped and protected us.

—You're ranting again, Jim.

—No, listen. Right down on a sense level, on a Pavlovian response level, we don't even turn to look anymore. Same thing with car alarms. Thing goes off, buzzers and bells, I mean some of these things are obnoxious as hell, and nobody even turns to look.

—Well, so often they trigger because somebody walked by with heavy boots on. They're too sensitive or something, they're going off all over the place. Thunder can do it, cat jumping on the car. People are already conditioned to ignore them because they normally don't mean anything is wrong. I know what you're saying, I mean what good are they if people ignore them but it doesn't portend the revelation or anything, Jimbo. Nothing insidious like the desensitization of modern man.

—I don't know. Is urban violence so prevalent that we don't even register it? This is a vision of the future not limited to science fiction writers. I mean *Blade Runner* wasn't too farfetched with its crowded prophecy of lights and smoke and no room to move around. I sometimes think a modern city is already the nightmare Wells or Verne or any of those turn-of-the-century seers saw.

—What's prefigured this?

—I don't know.

—Take a deep breath, big guy. It's not as dark by half as you want to believe. What's that quote, the times are never so bad that a good man can't thrive?

—Ok.

—What else?

—Nothing else. You know, I think it's Katey doing this to me.

—Do you mean Katya? You're not gonna obsess about my co-worker?

—No, dipshit. Katey. Like, you know, my youngest, my daughter. I've discovered a new vulnerability being the father of a little girl.

—Well, that's natural. But to let it color your whole worldview.

—Everything colors my worldview. That's what a worldview is.

—Everything negative. You gotta accentuate the optimistic...

—Oh, stop. And whaddya mean I'm not gonna obsess about your co-worker. I reserve the right to obsess.

—I know you, Jimbo. I've been there. Don't carry any kind of little confidential torch for this woman. Don't let it enter your environment, your comfortable nest. Don't let it affect your worldview.

—Right.

—How's Conrad, by the way?

—Fine, why?

—Oh, you said something last time about homework problems, or a bit of difficulty with one of his teachers.

—Oh, you know, the homework thing. I was never a good concentrator either. Smart enough but couldn't knuckle down, couldn't keep my focus. I'm not too distressed about the homework problem. The teacher, I don't know. You gotta realize your information is filtered through a ten year old's perspective. He says, she said, his project was junk.

—What teacher would be that harsh?

—Yeah, that's what I figure. She wouldn't use the word junk. He's gotten his feelings hurt by something she said, I imagine, and that colored her comments about the project, which, by the way, I thought, he'd done a fine job with.

—Well, should you go and talk to her?

—I don't know. I don't want to become one of that kind of parent, you know, who runs to the teacher at every little slight. I figure if I let it blow over and it blows over, well, it wasn't that big a deal in the first place. I don't want to magnify it by my interest.

—Very mature.

—Thank you. I can still sometimes pull off a good one. I don't have any big ideas but I've got a lot of good small ones.

—What's the big idea?

—Right. Exactly. Still I can sometimes pull off a good one.

—You can. Absolutely.

—Now about your co-worker?

*

—My throat's starting to hurt.

—I'm sorry. Take some echinacea.

—I did. It still hurts.

—Echinacea is not a remedy, it's a preventative.

—It's too late for echinacea then.

—Ok. Are you getting sick, you think? Everyone else has had it.

—I don't know. I think I'm on the outskirts of a cold.

—Can I get you anything?

—No. I'm just gonna lie here and watch this game.

—Ok. You know Connie's counting on you to set up that game with him.

—So I shouldn't lie here?

—Of course you should if you feel bad. I'm just saying.

—I know. Where is Connie?

—He's down at Brad's.

—So he's not too worried about getting that game set up today.

—I don't know. I think Brad had to go somewhere with his father later so Connie'll be home oneish.

—Alright.

—You don't have to do it.

—No, I want to. I will.

—I can do it.

—No, no. I got the darn thing for him. I want to. Lemme just vegetate here for a little.

—Ok. This is why you should stick to video games, there's nothing for adults to do. I think part of their very design is to disclude adults. Even if adults wanted to get involved they're chromosomally excluded.

—Hey, I can do that Turok one.

—Congratulations.

—Ok. But I got him this Weapons and Warriors thing to get Connie away from the TV screen for a little while. At least this game is a little closer to my past experience. My father always had to get down and help my brother and me set up some cockamamie thing we got for Christmas. Mousetrap or something.

—I thought you said your father never got down on the floor with you.

—Well, I sort of don't remember him, you know, physically down on the floor with us. But we got all these complex games, so he must have figured in the construction of them somehow. By the way, have you looked at this Weapons and Warriors thing. It's intimidating. There must be a thousand parts. All in these little baggies, separated by color and use. Little cannons, catapults, knights, I don't know whatall. I can't make head nor tails out of it. I only hope Connie can.

—Not much is wasted on Connie. Have we ever gotten him anything that he didn't eventually get interested in?

—I know. The Erector set.

—I bet he even comes around to that. Though I warned you he would find that too demanding. You only wanted him to have that because you had one.

—I didn't get him that. Grandma did.

—Because you told her to.

—Yeah, I guess that's right. My throat hurts. I don't want to talk anymore.

—Ok, sport. Gimme kiss and I'll leave you alone.

—Thanks.

—You want me to take Katey to Target or somewhere, let you sleep?

—Naw. Katey won't bother me. Where is she anyway?

—I don't know. It's too quiet. She's probably in our room emptying the box of wooden matches on the floor. Her favorite new game.

*

—Of course, I over-think everything. I *know* I over-think everything. It is what I do; it is my defining principle. Self-consciousness weighs heavily on my soul. I mean, if I go to the cabinet to get a glass I think, I'm picking out a glass for water and is this the glass that I want? Does it fit its function at this time? Or is that the glass I normally take an Alka-seltzer in and what if I use it now and it's dirty and I need to take an Alka-seltzer sometime soon? Is it too large for what I want right now, I mean, I only want a swallow of cranberry juice, do I really need that big glass? And the tumbler, my favorite glass, I have to calculate how many we have currently in the cabinet against how many drinks I may have today before we run the dishwasher again. The tumbler fits the hand so nicely, it's, what's the word, ergonometric. But do I want to waste a tumbler, knowing that we only have a finite number of tumblers, on this drink of milk, which I won't enjoy as much as the glass of decaf ice tea I will undoubtedly have later? There's so much to think about here it's a wonder I move at all. I mean, I really understand the fellow who goes rigid with indecision. Like the character in John Barth's *The End of the Road*, who becomes frozen because he has no compelling reason to get up, to put one foot in front of another. It's as if I have to have a good reason for doing *anything*. A compelling reason. It's emotional catatonia, death in life. It's a wonder I get out of bed in the morning, since, in order to do it, I have to think I need to get out of bed. And, sometimes, I lack the confidence to do that simple mental exercise, to set the body into motion, to wind up a new day and know that *anything* can happen, a day full of the terrible possibility of possibility.

*

—Oh, I couldn't go, you know. Couldn't travel. The farther I get from my home the more attenuated my nervous system. It's fragile elastic, my lifeline.

—But you used to travel, right? Used to sell books all over the midsouth.

—Yeah. I've gotten worse, which's the secret of it. I've gotten worse.

—What was it, you, what, couldn't stand sleeping alone?

—Nah. I'm used to sleeping alone, I'm married.

—Ha. Right.

—No, it was the, I don't know, the horrible aloneness of it, the total responsibility of acting as a free agent. It was like, if I didn't start the car, keep it straight between the lines, not stray into oncoming traffic, that kind of thing, I had no backup, you know? I mean it was my sole accountability.

—That's weird. Have you talked to anyone about this?

—Yes. You. Just now.

—Well, pal, I'm sort of not good enough. Really. You maybe ought to see someone.

—What my wife keeps saying. Do you think I'm crazy, or heading that way?

—Nah. Or not more than the rest of us. It's just, what, some switch or something is not making the proper connection, you know?

—You think it's that simple. Some medical man could throw that switch for me.

—No, nothing's that simple. Not a cough, not plantar's warts. I'm saying, you're not that bad off, I mean, you function day to day, you walk around, you sell books, and you're even pretty good at it. You're what they call high function. But, this depression, this mania you're developing, seems like it might be fairly commonplace, fairly easy to head off. What do I know? Why listen to me?

—No, no, I appreciate it. Maybe so, maybe so. But psychiatry, you know, it's kind of a religion, you have to have a sort of faith to even get started. I mean, I don't expect a bolt from the blue to manifest a deep religious feeling in me anymore than I expect some head-shrinker to find the key to my rusty lock. Life isn't *Three Faces of Eve*, you know what I mean, I didn't kiss my dead grandmother and I'm blocking that memory and if I didn't block that memory I would be cured.

—No. There's no cure in psychiatry; I'm with you there. It's an ongoing thing. What am I arguing, I don't believe anymore than you do. I'm just, um, concerned.

—Thanks. I know.

—You've had depression before, I mean, when you were younger, when we were in college. You sat out a year with it, didn't you?

—Sort of, yeah. It's different now, I don't know why. More deep seated, or something.

—What did you do back then to snap out of it?

—If I ever snapped out of it.

—Right.

—Met a new woman normally. I mean, I remember talking to this college counselor, nice woman in the psych department, my brother put her onto me, and she was trying to be very helpful and she asked, you know, what would make me happier, what would trigger a new reason to live, to get back to life-participation. And I remember being somewhat embarrassed by my answer but it was honest, I said, there's this woman in my sociology class.

—Eternal cure.

—Right. And when I think of that woman now, oh she was so fine, little turned up nose, beautiful body, I think of how depressed I was, I think of how I longed for her.

—But you never went out with her.

—You know, the queer thing about it is, I don't remember. I think we might have gone out but maybe it wasn't there, the chemistry or whatever.

—What was her name?

—Lynn.

—Not Lynn Leslie.

—No, I didn't meet Lynn Leslie till later.

—And you guys dated didn't you?

—No, I never dated Lynn Leslie. She was your fixation.

—Well. Yeah, I did have a crush on her.

—Right. Different Lynn.

—What was your Lynn's last name?

—I don't remember.

—Really. Do you remember kissing her, or more, do you remember anything physical?

—Kissing, maybe. I'm pretty sure we never did anything else. I think I'd remember. She had these tremendous breasts, still thinking about how they swelled her sweatshirt gives me palpitations.

—Do you really have women in your past with whom you were intimate but you can't remember their names, or faces, or whatever?

—Yes. Horrible, isn't it?

—Well.

—I know. I was fairly unruly, I realize, but the physical thing was, well, so important to me, back then and later, yes. Well, still, but I can't believe there are women who unlocked their secret places for me and I don't even remember their names. I'm horrible. I'm not worth spit.

—You're not so bad. Think. Come up with one.

—Oh, golly. You know, fairly recently, I was in the book store and this woman came in and she was, you know, somehow familiar and I could almost come up with her name, Terry, or Susan, or one of those names so common to my youth, and for a moment there I thought, oh my God I've slept with this woman and I'm not even sure whether I know her.

—Did you speak to her?

—Well, I answered her question.

—Which was?

—Do you have any A. S. Byatt?

—That's it?

—Yeah. Of course she didn't say anything either, so—

—Yeah, I guess so. Couldn't you look at her, you know her body and all and figure out whether she had ever gotten naked with you before?

—No, I really couldn't. Of course age changes us. She was moderately chunky, not unlike myself, and maybe transformed from the young willowy thing she was way back yonder.

—Yeah.

—You're disgusted with me. You judge.

—No, really. It's just, my past is so simple. There were four women. Four. I know all their names, remember all their familiarity. Christ, I even know where they are now and whom they're married to.

—Is this counting the tag team fuck you had one drunken teenage night?

—Oh, I've told you that.

—Of course you have. You've told me everything. Twenty-five years is a long time, friend.

—Yeah. I haven't told you everything, of course.

—Really?

—Well, I don't think so. Are you suggesting you've told me everything, every sordid little thing?

—Yeah, I think so.

—Huh.

—Yeah. I think I have.

—Huh.

—I even told you about my fling with the older married woman.

—That's not so horrible. A time honored situation, really.

—Yeah.

—Is that your worst? That little dalliance.

—I guess so. I guess I'm least proud of that, though God knows, there was a time when I really wanted her, morality be damned.

—That's how it goes, isn't it?

—Yeah. The body has reasons whereof the mind knows not. Or something.

—Yeah.

*

—And have you told Dorothea everything?

—What?

—You told me you've told me everything.

—Oh. Right. Well, Dorothea, of course not. She's my wife after all.

—But, I mean about before her.

—Oh, no, no. I mean, I don't think women, well, people, really want to hear all that shit, do you? About the past and all.

—But the point is, I'm, what, your confidant?

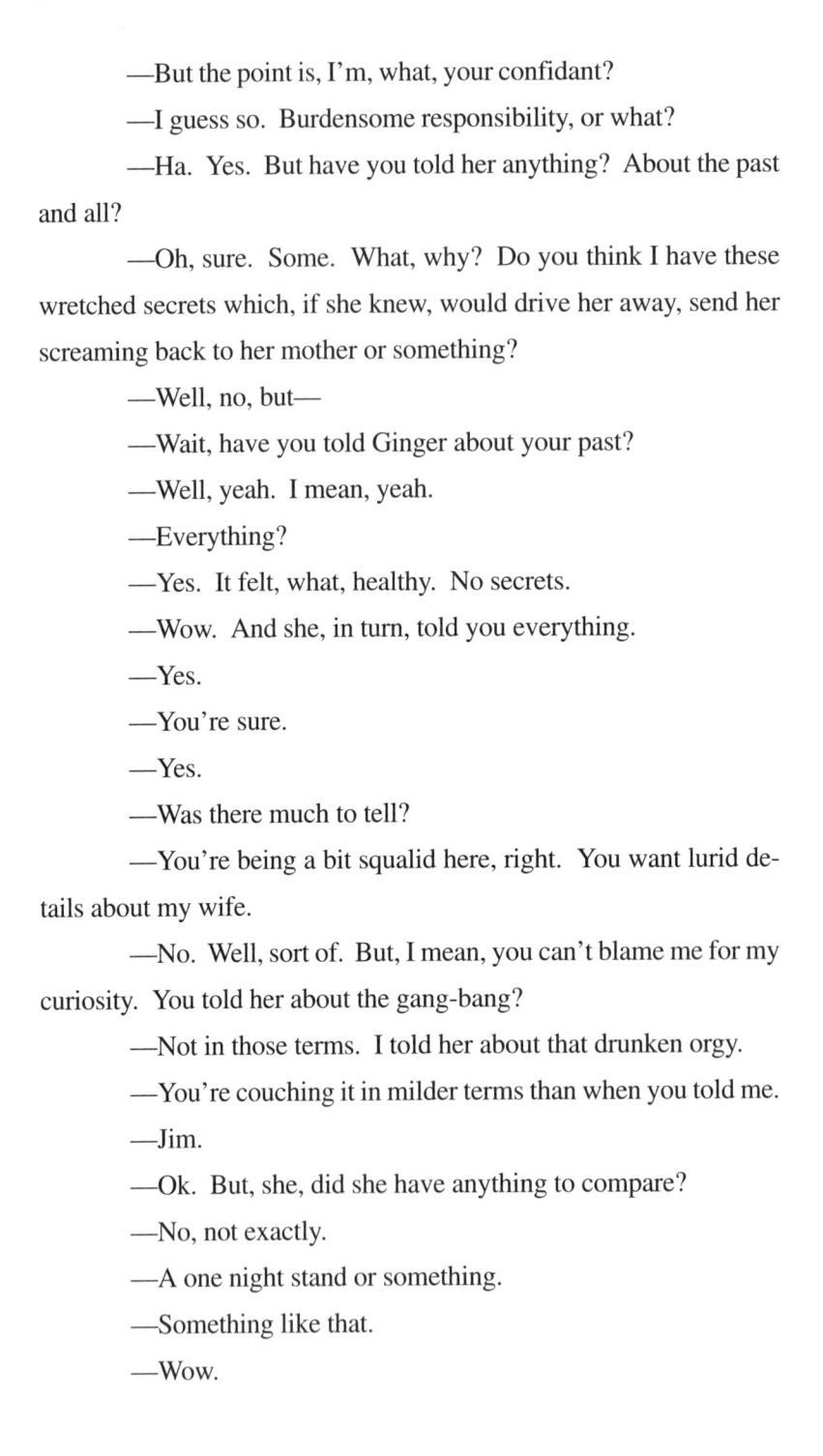

—I guess so. Burdensome responsibility, or what?

—Ha. Yes. But have you told her anything? About the past and all?

—Oh, sure. Some. What, why? Do you think I have these wretched secrets which, if she knew, would drive her away, send her screaming back to her mother or something?

—Well, no, but—

—Wait, have you told Ginger about your past?

—Well, yeah. I mean, yeah.

—Everything?

—Yes. It felt, what, healthy. No secrets.

—Wow. And she, in turn, told you everything.

—Yes.

—You're sure.

—Yes.

—Was there much to tell?

—You're being a bit squalid here, right. You want lurid details about my wife.

—No. Well, sort of. But, I mean, you can't blame me for my curiosity. You told her about the gang-bang?

—Not in those terms. I told her about that drunken orgy.

—You're couching it in milder terms than when you told me.

—Jim.

—Ok. But, she, did she have anything to compare?

—No, not exactly.

—A one night stand or something.

—Something like that.

—Wow.

—This surprises you.

—Well, yeah. I mean, Ginger, Jesus. She's so demure or something.

—Not really.

—You guys didn't get into like details or anything? Details are a bad idea between husband and wife.

—We have told all. We trust that we have told all.

—Hm. Orgasms and—

—Enough.

—Sorry. I didn't mean to embarrass you, I mean, it's Jim, buddy.

—Yeah. Well, she did allow that she hadn't had an orgasm before me.

—And you believe her.

—Yes. Why?

—Well—nothing. You told her about your brother's wife?

—Oh. Well, no. I didn't mention that.

—Ok then.

—But that's still sort of current, you know? I mean, we have to have dinner with them, etc.

—I understand. You told her about that night with Cindy and the camera—

—Nothing much happened that night.

—I know. We just got a little high and talked your girlfriend out of her shirt.

—Ha ha. Right. We did do that.

—That was some night.

—We have pictures.

—Ha ha. We do. Ha.

—Cindy. Jesus.

—She had some breasts, Cindy did.

—We have pictures.

—Ha ha.

—I think we could have done more that night.

—Really? Don't tell me that. I'll fantasize about that. That'll break my heart.

—We were pretty high.

—And Cindy? She would have done more.

—I think so.

—Damn. What, did she tell you she would have or what?

—Yeah, sort of.

—Bastard.

—What?

—You've known this all these years.

—Well, I mean, she was my girlfriend. I didn't want her to want to do more. It might have led to our early demise, my knowledge that she wanted to do more.

—Damn. Sorry.

—Doesn't matter now. Just, you know—

—Yeah. What did she say?

—Well, I mean, afterwards, we looked at the physical evidence of that night and we were laughing and I was a little jealous, I guess. But there was one picture of you with your shirt off and her right next to you and you look like, well, like you were fixing to jump on her.

—I probably was.

—And we were laughing, or she was, and she said, Jim liked my breasts. Kind of half question, half statement. And I said, sure and she said, what did he say, and I said, not much, but that, yes, he liked your breasts. And she says, kind of shy and mischievous, that was fun.

    —Fun. Jesus.

    —Yeah.

    —That's all.

    —Well.

    —Come on, dammit.

    —Well she said, I would have gone on.

    —Gone on.

    —Right, that's the phrase she used. Gone on. And I was like, Wow, and she said, Well, we were stoned and all and it would have been cool being naked with two men whom she liked so well.

    —Damn.

    —Right.

    —And you told Ginger this.

    —Yes.

    —Damn.

*

    —Art saves us. I know that's not original, but there it is. That's what I've figured out.

    —Huh.

    —Art saves us. How many times has a good book, song,

whatever, lifted you out of yourself, brought you back from the edge of alone.

—The edge of alone.

—Whatever. Listen. I was watching *Blume in Love* the other day.

—The Paul Mazurksy thing. I love that movie.

—I know you do. That's where I got the idea from. I'd never seen it and I knew you loved it.

—Huh.

—And it just sort of blossomed in me, this reaching out for contact, this expansiveness in me. I suddenly felt a part of humanity, connected, that's what I felt, connected.

—Through George Segal.

—Yeah. I mean it's a wonderful movie, you know. It's not Bergman but it's wonderful, kind of warm and smart and simple, really, but it made me feel good to be part of a species that creates things like that, movies like *Blume in Love*.

*

—I wanna be one of those people who embrace life, back-slappers, drink buyers, *bon vivants*. I do. I wanna make people around me happy to bask in the glow of my expansiveness. I wanna be that for my friends, my family, someone who radiates an appreciation for just *being,* you know, for just existing. But right now life has me backed into a corner. I don't know. I've set some kind of trap for myself and stepped into it.

—You don't really want to be that guy. How dull, how prosaic.

—Ok.

—You speak as if life were a predator, a physical predator.

—Yes, exactly. Exactly that. It is a predator. And somewhere along the line I began to act like prey, only like prey.

—Pray.

—I'll try. Prayer, maybe that's the answer.

—When all else fails.

—Yes.

*

—You Ok?

—Yeah, or no. I'm—antsy, depressed.

—You take a pill.

—Eh.

—Meaning no.

—I don't know.

—Jim, dear. Take a pill.

—I know.

—Take one.

—It's like, I don't know. I have this pill which if I took it every day I'd have a better life, a better time of it. If God offered you this why would you not take it? I could be calm, even, even feel better physically.

—And?

—And yet I have this trepidation. Do I want to be the kind of person who has to take a pill everyday to get by?

—Jim. Where does this come from? I don't have to spell it out for you. Depression is a disease—even as in dis-ease, lack of ease. There's no cure but you have something to help. You take a Tylenol when you have a headache.

—Reluctantly, even then.

—But Jim, please.

—I don't know. Something to do with my mother probably. If I told my mother I was on antidepressants she would purse her mouth in disgust, say something like, Oh, Jim, aren't you happy with your beautiful wife and kids?

—And yet she could have used a good drug herself?

—And how. But she never was on drugs, that I know of. I don't think anyone ever diagnosed her with depression, yet I know she's where I got it. She's the wicked gene that possesses me.

—So you know all this.

—Right. Would you like me better if I were the kind of person who used a pill as a daily crutch, who gave in to the weakness of relying on medication just to get by, just to venture out to the grocery store?

—You're all mixed up, sweet. When you have bad days take the pill. Christ, it infuriates me.

—I know. But bad days, you know, when's it a bad day and when's it just a little nervousness or a little dyspepsia or constipation.

—You don't know, you can't tell?

—Sometimes. Sometimes it all feels the same. I'm, you know, not in touch with my body. What's that called, somatic something?

—Maybe psychosomatic.

—Psycho, right. I'm gonna take a pill.

—Good.

—But you know there's a finite number of these and at some point that snippy receptionist at the doctor's office is gonna say, That's enough for you, bub.

—You're overthinking this. You're projecting.

—Would you really like me better if I were the kind of person who did not project? An unexamined life liver.

—Right. Take the pill, sweetheart. Then let's go for a walk.

—It's raining.

—It's not.

—It's going to.

*

—*Meet John Doe.*

—*Ball of Fire.*

—Ha. She was great in that. Um, *Double Indemnity.*

—Hands down. Don't need to continue.

—Continue anyway.

—Ok. Um, *Sorry Wrong Number.*

—Right. *Union Pacific.*

—She was in that?

—Yeah, I think so.

—I haven't seen that since high school. Saw it over at Sandra Lederer's house, late one night, and every one else in bed. Kissed lovely Sandra Lederer once, she had wool pants on—why would I remember that? Her pants didn't feel good, rough to my touch, I thought, she must be hot in those. Sandra's dead now, of course.

—Damn.

—Right.

—*Lady Eve.*

—Oh. Good one.

—Thank you.

—Henry Fonda, man. Young and handsome and playing a genial rube. Gotta love it.

—Right.

—Let's do someone else.

—Ok. Thomas Mitchell.

—Oo. *Gone With the Wind.*

—Yeah, obvious. Not anywhere near his best.

—He was great in *Gone with the Wind.*

—Ok.

—He was.

—Ok. *It's a Wonderful Life.*

—Obvious.

—Stop it.

—*Mr. Smith Goes to Washington.*

—Was he in that?

—Wasn't he?

—Well, he should have been if he wasn't.

—What else?

—Let's do someone else.

—Chicken.

—Robert Vaughn.

—Ha. You know I was the world's biggest *Man from UNCLE* fan?

—Yes, I know.

—I had the plastic model. Came in two kits. One was Ilya jumping over a wall and the other was a continuation of the wall and Napoleon kneeling in front of it with, I don't know, a Mannlicher in his hand.

—A what?

—I don't know, a spy gun.

—Right.

—Movies, though, huh? Um, *Julius Caesar.*

—Good. *Superman*, uh, *3.*

—Right, he was in that. Good. *Bud the Chud.*

—Ha, ha. *Bud the Chud 2*, I believe.

—You're right.

—*Magnificent Seven.*

—Oh, man. I can't think of any others.

—Ok, best James Coburn.

—Oh, lawdy mama. I love James Coburn.

—Ok. *Duck You Sucker.*

—I love *Duck You Sucker.* It had another name, too, I think. Re-released under another name. Oh, wait. *Fistful of Dynamite.* But, wait, best by a landslide: *The President's Analyst.*

—Wow. Best sixties movie.

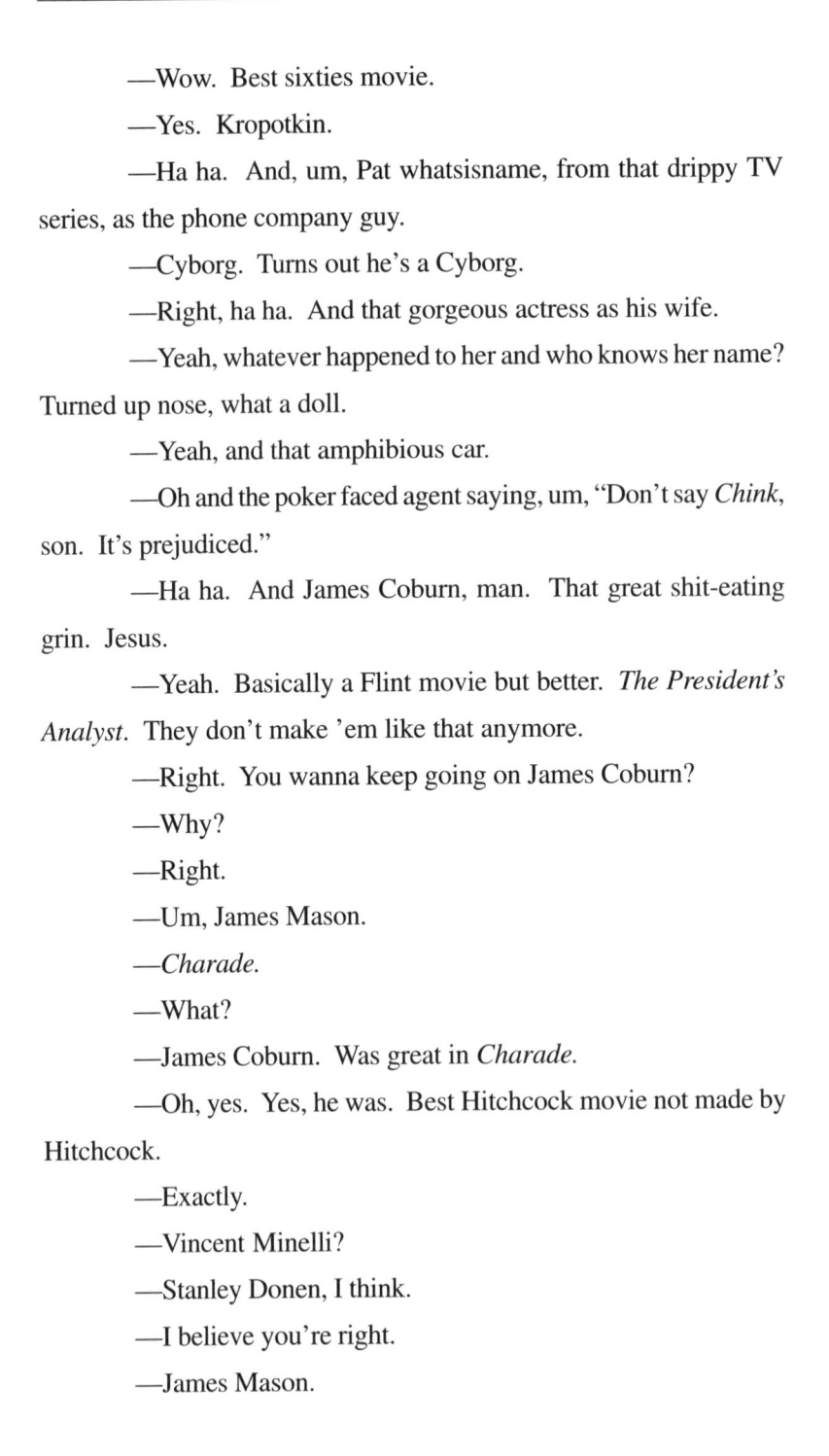

—Yes. Kropotkin.

—Ha ha. And, um, Pat whatsisname, from that drippy TV series, as the phone company guy.

—Cyborg. Turns out he's a Cyborg.

—Right, ha ha. And that gorgeous actress as his wife.

—Yeah, whatever happened to her and who knows her name? Turned up nose, what a doll.

—Yeah, and that amphibious car.

—Oh and the poker faced agent saying, um, "Don't say *Chink*, son. It's prejudiced."

—Ha ha. And James Coburn, man. That great shit-eating grin. Jesus.

—Yeah. Basically a Flint movie but better. *The President's Analyst*. They don't make 'em like that anymore.

—Right. You wanna keep going on James Coburn?

—Why?

—Right.

—Um, James Mason.

—*Charade*.

—What?

—James Coburn. Was great in *Charade*.

—Oh, yes. Yes, he was. Best Hitchcock movie not made by Hitchcock.

—Exactly.

—Vincent Minelli?

—Stanley Donen, I think.

—I believe you're right.

—James Mason.

—Nah.

—Wanna do favorite Woodstock stage announcements?

—Nah, I'm too tired now. Fucking James Coburn. Let's go home and rent *The President's Analyst*.

—Ok. Your house.

—Nah, kids are asleep.

—Can't go to mine.

—Well to hell with it.

—Right.

—Heather Graham.

—Thank you.

*

—Hi. I didn't recognize you at first.

—Hi. It's the hat. Here.

—Ah, yes. That's you.

—Yep.

—What are you doing? Mark give you the day off?

—Yes. I mean, no Thursday's always my day off.

—So, what brings you into the fuscous atmosphere of my bookstore. Surely not looking for a book?

—Why not? I read.

—A weak joke. I was being, what, breezy.

—Oh.

—So. What book?

—I don't know. Recommend something. Something good.

—Oh, something good. Let's see. That narrows it down quite a bit.

—Funny. Mark was telling me about some book, something about a magician, maybe.

—Magician. Oh, that's Robertson Davies, *World of Wonders*. Yeah, he's been reading that.

—How about that?

—Well, let's see. Yeah, we have it. But, look. That's the third book in a trilogy. You need to start with the first book, *Fifth Business*, which is favorable, because *Fifth Business* is only one of the best books of our time. But they're all in this one volume, conveniently packaged together by our friends at Penguin.

—Cripes.

—Cripes?

—I don't know if I want to commit to a whole trilogy. What if I don't like the first book.

—Money back guarantee.

—Really?

—Oh, sure. But you're gonna love *Fifth Business*, see? Either that or I never speak to you again.

—Ok.

—Whaddya mean, you don't want to commit to a trilogy. You on your way to some secret mission from which you might not return? Or you have a trouble with, you know, commitment in general?

—Don't get me started. Commitment, hm. It's overrated, isn't it?

—I don't know. Look, it's twelve ninety-four.

—A bargain for, what did you say, the greatest novel of our time?

—One of. Yes, a bargain.

—Well, thanks.

—Ok.

—I'll let you know what I think.

—Ok.

—

—Anything else?

—Um, no. I guess not.

—You know, you really do look like Ally Mc—

—Ugh. Please.

—It's the eyes.

—I know.

—And the, well—

—Perky ass?

—Well.

—I hear it. Believe me.

—I'll bet you do. Every joker in the bar who owns a TV.

—I don't frequent bars, but, yes. Surprising how many men think telling you you resemble the current cutesy in the public eye will get them an immediate in.

—Sorry.

—No, no. I know you didn't mean it that way.

—Well.

—You're married and all.

—And all. Yes.

—Mark says your wife is a real sweetheart.

—He's right, she is. Yes.

—Well.

—Ok, then. You'll tell me what you think of the Davies.

—Yes, I will. I'm going home to start it right now.

—Ok, then.

—Goodbye.

—Goodbye. See you soon.

*

—You want onions on yours?

—We always have onions.

—Right.

—Aren't you gonna have em? I'll cut some if you don't want any.

—No, no. Have you ever thought though that a dog won't eat an onion? Drop a piece of onion on the floor and old Fido will sniff it and let it lie. I mean, what does that mean? Dogs'll eat feces but an onion they turn away from. I think there's a message there for us.

—Eat feces?

—Funny. No, I mean maybe God never meant us to eat onions.

—God, huh?

—Well, I mean, the plan, you know, if there's a plan. We should pay more attention to nature. You know the, what, macrobiotics only eat food grown in their region. You know, like if tomatoes only come from exotic warm locales and you live like in Minnesota you wouldn't eat tomatoes.

—But if onions grew in your region.

—Ok, I'm just thinking out loud.

—You wanna test this food on Fly first?

—No.

—You gonna cut an onion?

—Sure.

—You're in a funny frame of mind.

—Am I?

—Seemingly. Everything go all right at work today? Any interesting new novels?

—Yeah, I mean no on the novels. We got the new Joyce Carol Oates.

—Has another week gone by already?

—Right.

—Nothing else?

—Um, new biography of Solzhenitsyn.

—Like you care.

—Like I care. Oh, I know. The Doug Hobbie came in in paperback.

—Good book.

—Yes. I'm gonna try to push it in paperback. I didn't have much luck with the hardcover edition.

—Funny how hard it is to get people interested in some authors no matter how good they are.

—Therein lies one of the great mysteries of this queer business I find myself in.

—What about the Philip Roth?

—What about it, you mean like am I selling it?

—Yeah.

—Some. Always hard to push Roth. I mean, I loved that book, well, loved his last four books, but there's this prejudgment thing going on with Roth, a sort of unexamined handed-down truth which has nothing to do with truth. You know, like he's dirty, or he's sexist or whatever. Like Hemingway. Getting women to read Hemingway is like pulling teeth. All they know is he shot animals, swaggered, fucked a lot. They don't know the magisterial beauty of his sentences, or how tender he can be.

—Well, I see what you're saying. I still don't like Hemingway.

—I know you don't.

—You know, Connie's writing a story again?

—You're kidding. What a kid. Something about aliens?

—No, I think this one is about you.

—Oh my goodness. What do you know?

—Only that the hero is named Jim.

—Oh my goodness.

—Yes.

*

—Book Shoppe.

—

—Hello, hey.

—

—Yes, I know. How are you?

—

—Oh, good. I told you.

—

—Well, the second's not quite as good as *Fifth Business*, but so few books are.

—

—Oh, yeah. Well, it's kind of a case of diminishing returns. The third is not quite as good as the first or second. Well, I don't know. I have a friend who prefers the third book to the other two, so there you go.

—

—Yes.

—

—Well, when you're done I'll tell you what I think about how all three mesh, or don't.

—

—The stone, yes.

—

—Uh huh. Well, I can recommend something, I'm sure.

—

—Ok. Glad you called.

—

—Nothing, just, you know. Good to talk books. Love to recommend books.

—

—Ok.

—

—Yeah, bye-bye.

*

—What's going on this next week? Anything?

—Nothing special, why? You going to P&H with Mark Friday as usual?

—No. I mean, probably. I was thinking of taking Thursday off instead of Saturday.

—Ok. How come?

—Oh, Saturday's sales have been sluggish. I thought I'd go in, see what happens on these lazy weekends.

—You think Dara and Jeff are slacking off?

—No, not exactly. Just, you know, thought I'd work a coupla weekends see if I can see anything wrong, anything I can do to stimulate sales.

—Sounds like a good idea. Maybe I'll take the kids to the zoo, then.

—Connie still like the zoo? He's seemed sort of indifferent to it the last few times we went.

—Yeah, he mopes a bit. But I think he really likes it. He just doesn't like walking around much. Be good for him. Get out in the sun.

—Yeah, I think so. Get him away from Turok.

—Yeah. What are you going to do on Thursday then?

—I don't know, why? Read. Maybe write a bit.

—You writing again?

—No.

—But you want to start?

—Right.

—Good.

*

—Hi.

—Hi. What a surprise.

—Yeah, well.

—You wanna come in?

—Sure.

—Aren't you supposed to be at work?

—No, I switched my days off this week.

—Well, come in, sit down.

—Nice place.

—Jesus, it's a mess. If I'da known—

—No, no. I'm sure I can find a place to sit. This coffee cup, you drank this, when?

—Gimme that, smartass. I just haven't had enough dishes to fill the dishwasher in a while. You ever live alone?

—It's been a while.

—Right. Married and all.

—Ha. Yes.

—You're married and all.

—Right.

—So, why are you here?

—You always so to-the-point?

—Yes. No. It makes me nervous you showing up like this.

—Me too.

—So?

—Well, I mean, you know. Obviously I think you're very attractive.

—Yes. And me you.

—Really?

—You playing dumb?

—No.

—Ok then.

—It's just, you know.

—I don't. I most assuredly don't.

—Why am I here? Well—

—You wanna go to bed with me.

—Gulp.

—Ha. You look stricken.

—Well. Yes, I mean, I do, but, you know, I can't.

—And you came by to tell me that?

—No. I don't know.

—Here. Lemme sit too. Lemme sit close to you and we'll see if our nerves will allow us to talk.

—Ok.

—You all right?

—I'm feeling a little sick, actually. Suddenly.

—Really?

—Yeah. Nauseous. Oo.

—You wanna lie down?

—No, I. Mmm. Maybe I just better go.

—Ok.

—I'm sorry. This is—

—It's Ok.

—Ok. Sorry.

—All right.

—Well, bye then.

—Bye. We must do this again some time.

*

—I'm feeling poorly, mate.

—I'm sorry.

—Feeling lowly sunk into myself.

—You sick?

—Only in my pitiful head.

—Same thing? The depression, etc.?

—No. Sort of.

—What?

—Remember in *Clockwork Orange*? Remember the Ludovico technique, how they made Little Alex a celibate robot? Anytime he even contemplated anything evil or destructive or sexually depraved he would become violently ill, retch and urp and become then docile?

—And inadvertently they programmed him to respond that way to Beethoven.

—Right. I think I've been Ludovicoed.

—How do you mean?

—I'm just programmed to run on this even keel and if I vary even a millimeter I'm doomed. Doomed to panic attack or nausea or whatever the hell the doctor thinks is happening to me.

—Jesus, Jim. You think these pills are good for you?

—I don't know. You know I can take them and do all right. I just, you know, don't relish taking one every time I'm going to do anything besides sit in my house and read.

—Well, it's just a bad patch. You know, hang on and get through it. There's always light at the end of the tunnel.

—Is there?

—I don't know. Sometimes life is just hanging on, just getting by.

—Yeah.

—Anything special happen to upset your apple cart this week?

—Hm, no. No no.

—I'm sorry, man. I wish I could do something.

—Thanks.

—You guys want to come over soon, have dinner with Ginger and me?

—Sure.

2

"And if everything is so nebulous about a matter so elementary as the morals of sex, what is there to guide us in the more subtle morality of all other personal contacts, associations, and activities? Or are we meant to act on impulse alone? It is all a darkness."

—Ford Maddox Ford
from *The Good Soldier*

—You're back.

—Yes.

—Come in please.

—I thought, you know, last time went so well, you'd be dying to see me again.

—Come in and sit.

—You've cleaned up.

—Some.

—Looks nice.

—Thank you.

—My, aren't we formal?

—Right.

—So.

—So?

—I'm really sorry about last time.

—It's Ok. And, actually, I did want to see you again.

—Really?

—Yes. Crazy, isn't it? Humans are crazy.

—Yes. Listen.

—Ok.

—I've been thinking.

—Oh boy.

—We can't have an affair.

—This is where we were last week. You've come again to tell me the same thing. You're presuming I want to have an affair with a married man.

—Oh, Jesus. That's right, I am. Jesus. It sounds so sordid put that way, ay?

—Yes. But presume away.

—Meaning?

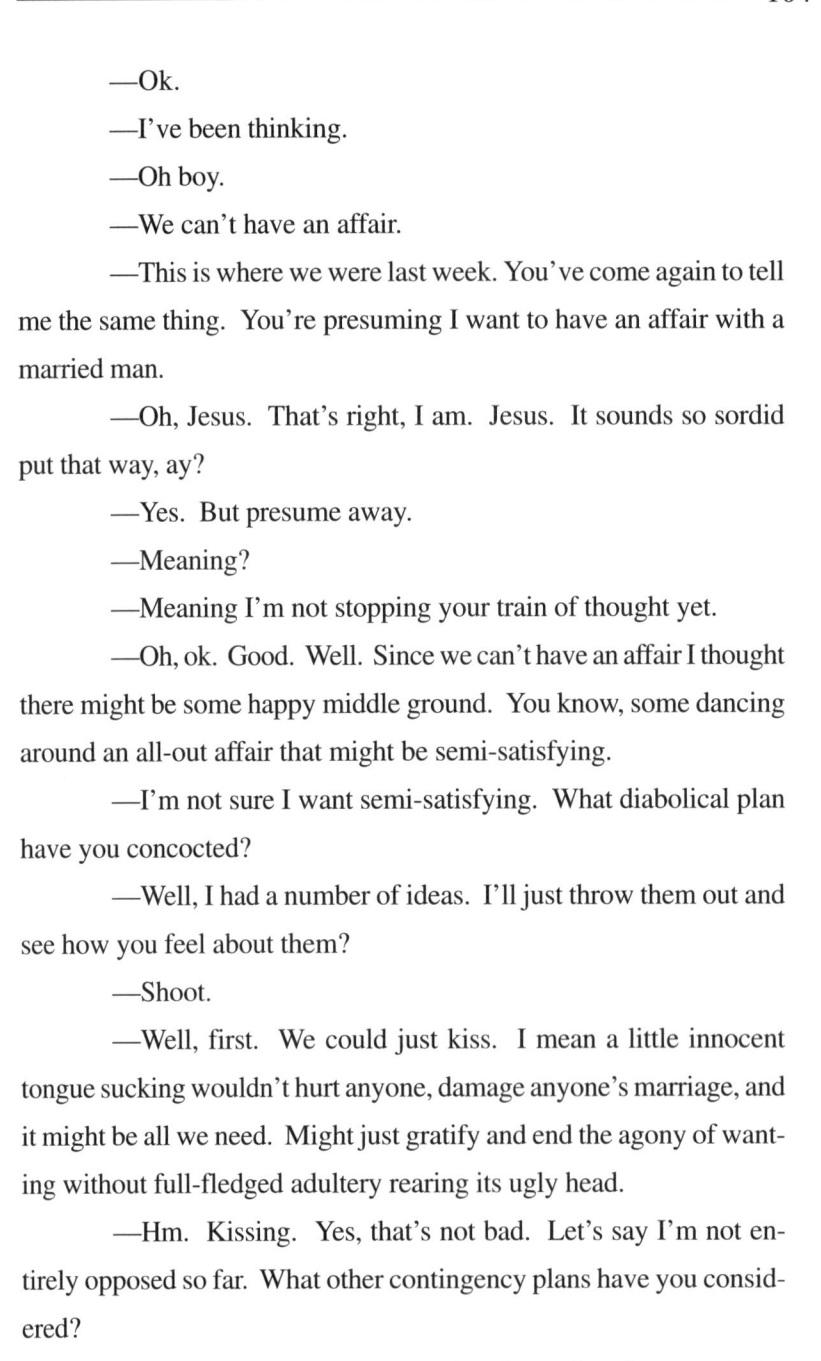

—Meaning I'm not stopping your train of thought yet.

—Oh, ok. Good. Well. Since we can't have an affair I thought there might be some happy middle ground. You know, some dancing around an all-out affair that might be semi-satisfying.

—I'm not sure I want semi-satisfying. What diabolical plan have you concocted?

—Well, I had a number of ideas. I'll just throw them out and see how you feel about them?

—Shoot.

—Well, first. We could just kiss. I mean a little innocent tongue sucking wouldn't hurt anyone, damage anyone's marriage, and it might be all we need. Might just gratify and end the agony of wanting without full-fledged adultery rearing its ugly head.

—Hm. Kissing. Yes, that's not bad. Let's say I'm not entirely opposed so far. What other contingency plans have you considered?

—Well, good. I feel heartened. These plans increase in intensity, so if they begin to threaten you hold up a palm.

—Check.

—Two. We could resort to the age-old flirting technique, which has served many a reluctant couple in eras, passed. The time honored back rub. Now this can be administered with as little sensuality as desired. With shirt, without shirt. Just in underwear. Just panties.

—You've given this a lot of thought.

—Well, yes. Guilty.

—I like plan 2. They get better?

—Well. Number 3 is a little more risqué, a little more embarrassing. Perhaps we could start with 1 or 2 and if we still needed more interim activity to short circuit the desire for an affair we could move on to Plan 3. I'm a little embarrassed to talk about it.

—You intrigue me. Please continue.

—Really?

—Tell me the plan, lunkhead. I'm getting a little excited here.

—Mm. Plan 3 would be, and this is a last ditch effort to stave off an affair, mind you. Plan 3 would be when the barbarians are at the gate, when all else has failed and all diplomatic routes have been undertaken and foundered and abandoned. Ship would be basically sinking, captain pacing around making peace with his personal gods, questioning the down-with-the-ship dictum, looking for face- and life-saving loopholes. Eleventh hour and the courier with the blueprint for deliverance tucked away in his pouch has been captured and is just then being tortured and, well, basically, is lost for all intents and purposes, no good for the reclamation of the mission—

—Ahem, as they say in the comic books.

— Plan 3 would be watching each other masturbate.

—Oh my.

—Sorry. I went too far.

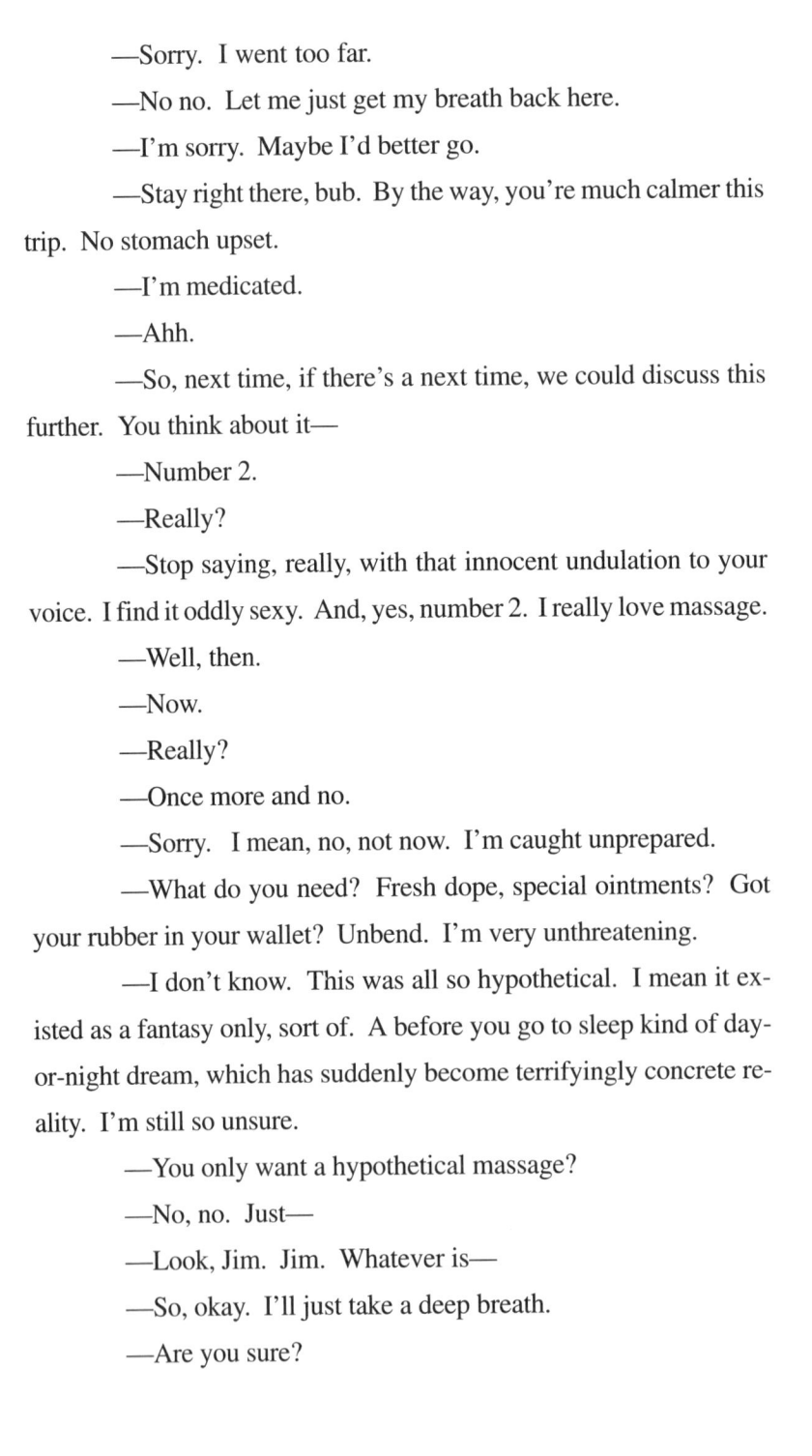

—No no. Let me just get my breath back here.

—I'm sorry. Maybe I'd better go.

—Stay right there, bub. By the way, you're much calmer this trip. No stomach upset.

—I'm medicated.

—Ahh.

—So, next time, if there's a next time, we could discuss this further. You think about it—

—Number 2.

—Really?

—Stop saying, really, with that innocent undulation to your voice. I find it oddly sexy. And, yes, number 2. I really love massage.

—Well, then.

—Now.

—Really?

—Once more and no.

—Sorry. I mean, no, not now. I'm caught unprepared.

—What do you need? Fresh dope, special ointments? Got your rubber in your wallet? Unbend. I'm very unthreatening.

—I don't know. This was all so hypothetical. I mean it existed as a fantasy only, sort of. A before you go to sleep kind of day-or-night dream, which has suddenly become terrifyingly concrete reality. I'm still so unsure.

—You only want a hypothetical massage?

—No, no. Just—

—Look, Jim. Jim. Whatever is—

—So, okay. I'll just take a deep breath.

—Are you sure?

—I think so.

—Am I massaging you or you me?

—Oh. I guess I always pictured it with me doing you.

—Suits me.

—Ok. Now degree of sensuality.

—I'm going to remove everything except my panties. How's that?

—Christ. You sure you don't wanna just make out?

—I'm opting for Number 2.

—Right.

—Ok then.

—I should just, what, turn my back and then you lie down.

—Ok. If you prefer.

—I'm nervous.

—I know.

—Tell me when you're ready.

—Ok.

—Ok. Jesus. I thought you were ready, like lying face down.

—No, I meant, ok I'll tell you when I'm ready.

—Oh. Jesus. You disrobe rapidly.

—Don't faint.

—No, no. It's just, look at what you've been hiding.

—My breasts are bigger than they look when I'm clothed. It's these athletic bras.

—Wow. I mean, you're beautiful. Ally McBeal with knockers.

—Ok. I'm lying down now.

—Ok. My you're lovely.

—Thank you. Come here.

—Right. You have a lovely back.

—Ok. Just start your work there, bucko.

—Right. Mm. Smooth.

—Mmm, that's nice. You have nice hands.

—

—

—Mm.

—You have, have a lovely ass.

—Mmm. You're not supposed to be looking there. Clinical, remember. This is just a back rub. Where's your professionalism?

—Right.

—Mm.

—You like me to rub your thighs?

—Mm hm.

—You have lovely thighs.

—Mm.

—Mmm.

—Oh my.

—Too close?

—No. Mmm.

—I'm just gonna rub a little bit under your panties band here, like so.

—Oh. Oh my.

—Mm, your ass. I, I just.

—Oh, that's nice. Pull them down.

—I.

—Yes. Pull them down.

—O.

—You, oh, want me to, mm, take them all the way off?

—Oh, oh goodness. Oh, your ass is soft.

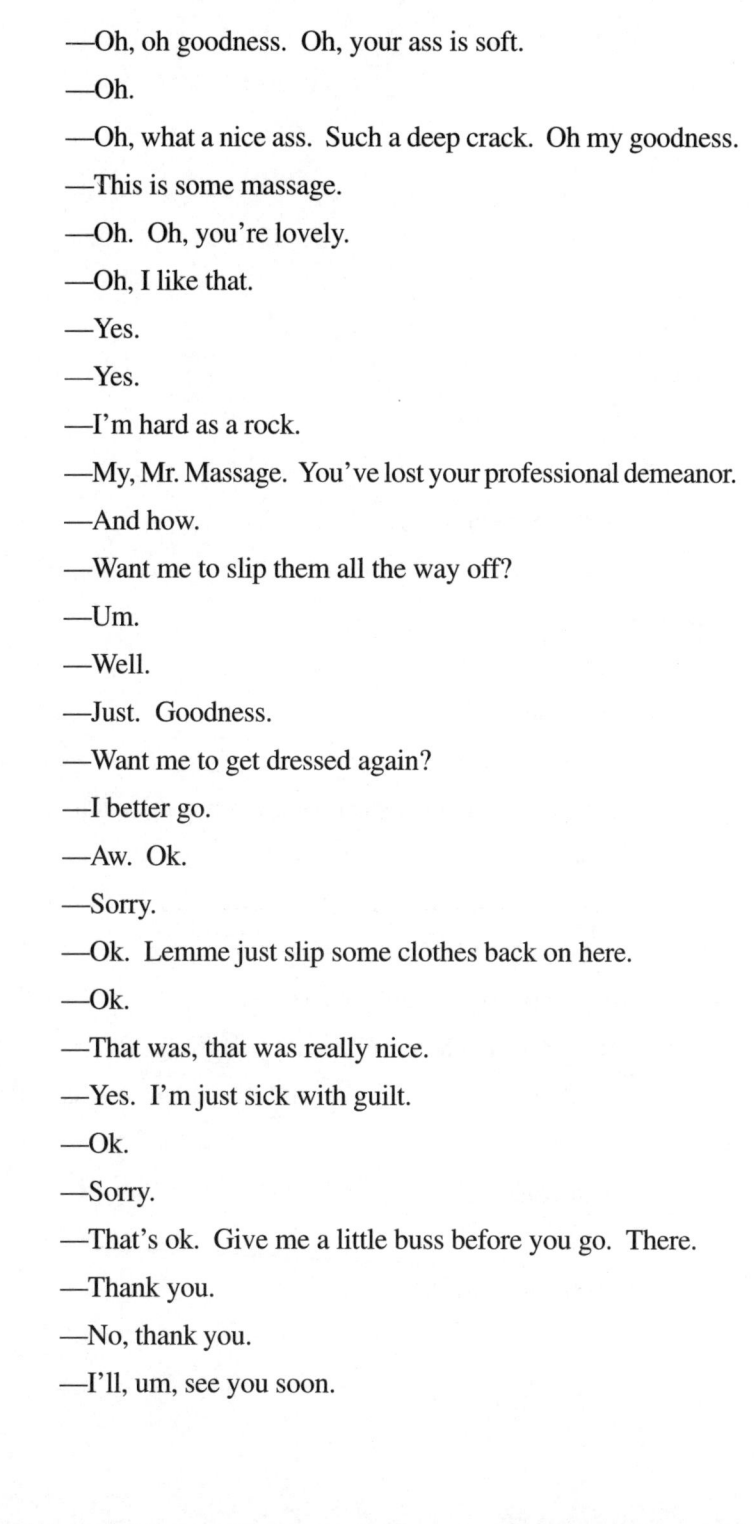

—Oh.

—Oh, what a nice ass. Such a deep crack. Oh my goodness.

—This is some massage.

—Oh. Oh, you're lovely.

—Oh, I like that.

—Yes.

—Yes.

—I'm hard as a rock.

—My, Mr. Massage. You've lost your professional demeanor.

—And how.

—Want me to slip them all the way off?

—Um.

—Well.

—Just. Goodness.

—Want me to get dressed again?

—I better go.

—Aw. Ok.

—Sorry.

—Ok. Lemme just slip some clothes back on here.

—Ok.

—That was, that was really nice.

—Yes. I'm just sick with guilt.

—Ok.

—Sorry.

—That's ok. Give me a little buss before you go. There.

—Thank you.

—No, thank you.

—I'll, um, see you soon.

—Ok.

*

—Hi.

—I'd like to sell these.

—Uh, let's see. We don't really buy much of this. . . . Perhaps—

—Your sign says you buy books.

—Yes, but—

—That's false advertising.

—Certainly you understand we can't buy everything.

—You should change your sign.

—Ok.

—How about $10 for the whole lot?

—I'm sorry. I just can't use them.

—You're a hard man. What can you give me?

—Nothing. I'm sorry. We can't use them. Perhaps Book Bank—

—Nothing?

—Right.

—You don't buy books.

*

—So this guy comes in today and he's got a handful of books to sell.

—Did you remember to call Stacey about doing our tax return?

—Am I telling a story here?

—Sorry, go ahead.

—This guy comes in—

—I got that part, he's selling books.

—Right. And he pulls out, you know, an Almanac from 1983, a, I don't know, a Reader's Digest Condensed with like an Irving Wallace and a Peter Benchley in it, a couple of mass markets look like they've been read by a couple dozen school kids and an old Latin textbook. Ok?

—So you told him his tastes were abysmal and sent him packing.

—Thanks. No, I kindly told him he didn't have anything we needed but we appreciated him thinking of us.

—Of course you said that.

—Are you being unnecessarily downputting tonight?

—Downputting? Is that a verb?

—Never mind.

—Oh, finish the anecdote. I'm sorry.

—So he gets indignant, right? He says, your sign says you buy books.

—Ha. I guess he thought he had you there.

—Right. And I allowed as to how we don't buy everything, but he's pissed and he goes out the door muttering and cursing and grumbling how he'll take his business elsewhere. I felt like chasing him down and pressing him about how much business he's done with us in the past. I mean I'd never seen this joker before but he's suddenly irate with me and leveraging me with a threat never to bring me his musty refuse ever again. I was a might steamed.

—Of course you were. Tell me again why you love retail.

—I know. But, of course, I don't love retail. I just love selling books.

—I know.

—It's like those kids who come in and ask for a student discount on their textbooks. I'm like, who else is going to buy textbooks? Everybody's looking for an edge all the time everywhere. Where did people get this idea that the world owes them a favor?

—I know. I don't know.

—Where are our kids?

—Connie's down at Ethan's. Katey, I don't know. Katey?

—Katey's in our room playing with lipstick.

—You're kidding.

—No. I mean, you know, chapstick, which she calls lipstick.

—If you knew where she was why did you ask me?

—It was just, you know, phatic filler, conversational gambits intended to keep a flow going.

—Right.

—And I did call Stacey. Her number's been disconnected.

—Oh, great.

—I know. I'll do the taxes.

—Uh oh.

—Whaddya mean? I can do it.
—I'll do them.
—Ok.

*

—Hello, princess.
—Daddy, I'm not gonna pull Flydog's tail.
—Ok.
—I'm not.
—I know you're not. You don't want to hurt the dog.
—We don't pull dogs' tails.
—That's right.
—We don't hurt dogs.
—That's right.
—Daddy, is Halloween coming again?
—Yes, princess.
—Is Halloween coming again?
—That's right. It'll be a while.
—And we're gonna get big big big big candy.
—Yes.
—We're gonna trick or treat.
—Yes.
—And Connie will be an alien.
—If he wants again.

—And I'm gonna be Tinky Winky.

—If you'd like.

—And Santa Claus is gonna bring us lots of candy.

—Um, right.

—I'm good. I'm not a bad girl.

—No, you're not.

—And I'm gonna get big big big candy.

—Ok.

—We don't pull dogs' tails.

—That's right. That's right, princess.

*

—I'll tell you what I really think. Murderers, rapists, fetishists, um, child molesters—I fear they are just the way God made them. You know, I, I'm profligate, sexually, emotionally. I was. I gave away my heart helter-skelter, my seed distributed hither and yon, when I was younger. I was like a fertilizer spreader, a renegade firehose. But, it's chemical, you know, it's brain connections, synapses, electronic impulses, I don't know whatall. I can't help wanting women, many women, variety. It's like that Woody Allen thing, you know, there are a million sperm and one egg, of course men stray. Regardless of how happy, how secure I am. And, I forgive myself this way. I know there are women I've hurt, some I fear, irreparably. I mean I can point to some lives which took bad turns, possibly, and I insist on the *possibly*, because of my turning away at an improper time, my wanton disregard of the sanctity of a monogamous relationship, my libertine take on sexual mores. But that desire, that root deep desire, never waned, that tug toward other flesh, no matter how forbidden, that, *that* never suffered a setback. Jesus, when my dad was in the hospital with his first heart attack, I was shaking with grief and dread, and yet, there was this woman in the hospital corridor. I know. It's horrible, pitiful. But, what I'm saying is, I fear the plan allows for this. I am the way my maker made me. This licentious drive, this grivoiserie, was built in. I think, maybe, and this is a buried consternation that it's the same way with, you know, the dreck of mankind, the Richard Specks, the Berkowitzes, the Hitlers, maybe. I guess I mean, I *hope* the plan allows for this. For all this. No one can help how they are, what they are. From the woman who comes gibbering into the bookstore about the devil to the guy whose freezer holds hidden, frozen outrages. It's all chemical. It's all factory installed.

—And this makes it innocent?

—I don't know. It makes it part of the pattern, the, um, plan.

—Again with the plan. When did you become so religious?

—Is it religious to think that all human activity is inherently inculpable because ordained by a higher power. I guess it is. Is this what I believe? It sounds horrible. But it's what I shudder at, it's my fear that this is so.

—And you are forgiving yourself for what?

—Oh, no. Nothing. I mean, everything. Nothing specific.

—Hey, Jimbo. This is Mark, right?

—Nothing really. I'm just making speculation here. Just feeling my way around in my cell.

—Ok.

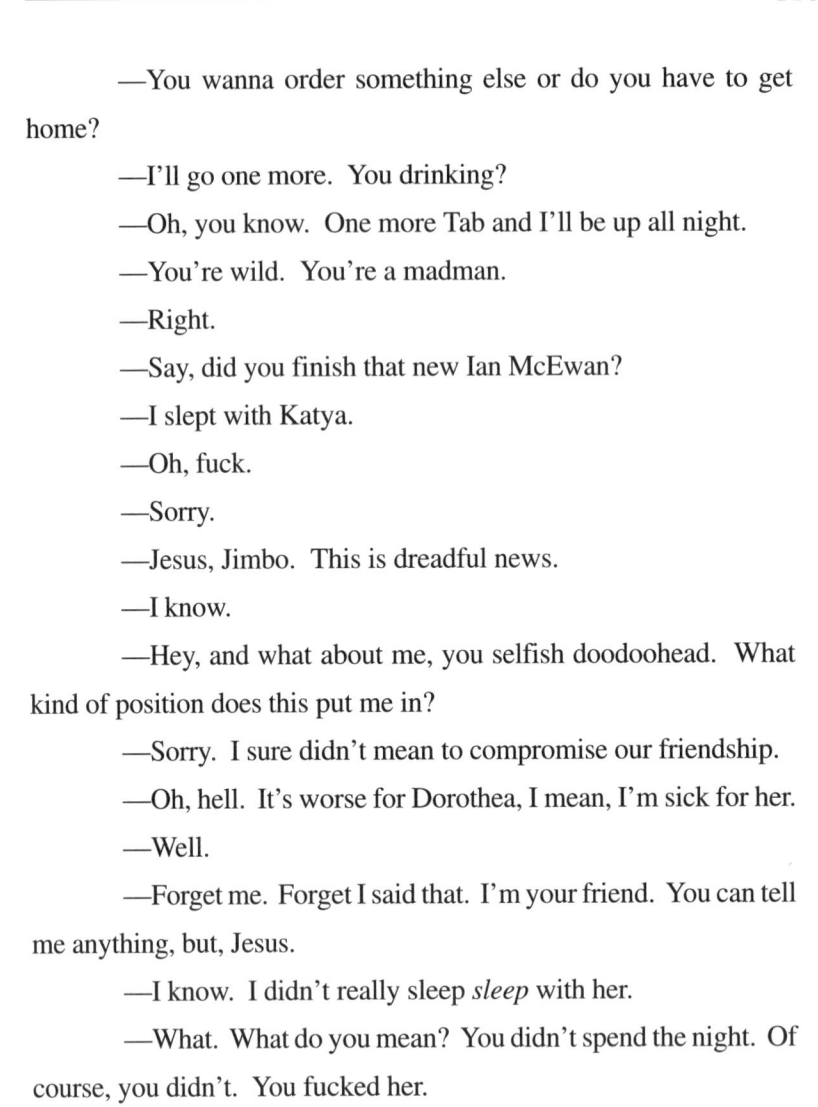

—You wanna order something else or do you have to get home?

—I'll go one more. You drinking?

—Oh, you know. One more Tab and I'll be up all night.

—You're wild. You're a madman.

—Right.

—Say, did you finish that new Ian McEwan?

—I slept with Katya.

—Oh, fuck.

—Sorry.

—Jesus, Jimbo. This is dreadful news.

—I know.

—Hey, and what about me, you selfish doodoohead. What kind of position does this put me in?

—Sorry. I sure didn't mean to compromise our friendship.

—Oh, hell. It's worse for Dorothea, I mean, I'm sick for her.

—Well.

—Forget me. Forget I said that. I'm your friend. You can tell me anything, but, Jesus.

—I know. I didn't really sleep *sleep* with her.

—What. What do you mean? You didn't spend the night. Of course, you didn't. You fucked her.

—No, no. I mean I balked. I wanted to, but I didn't. We just kind of, you know, innocently fooled around.

—Innocently.

—Shit, I know. We just kind of did some rubbing and feeling and, I don't know what I'm doing.

—So there was no, no, you know, baring peepees.

—Ha. No. We, I, balked. I couldn't continue. We tried this

silly compromise, you know, a sensual backrub instead of going to bed.

—But in bed.

—Well, technically.

—Jimbo, there are no compromises. You're either a creep or you're not.

—Really?

—No, I guess not. I don't exactly believe in Jimmy Carter's lust in the heart thing. But, Jesus, are you gonna do it again?

—No. No, I'm really gonna try not to.

—Good boy.

—Ok.

—Look, I'm no one to talk. You know. I, I've lusted after some women since Ginger, but—

—But you never acted on it.

—I guess that's the distinction.

—Yeah.

—So, I hope this doesn't make it awkward for me with Katya at the office.

—I hope so, too. Are you sorry I told you?

—No, no. You know, we're like, you know, brothers.

—Thanks.

—Shit.

—I know.

—Well, anyway.

—She has the smoothest ass. It's like velvet.

—Oh, Jesus. Don't talk about it.

—Ok. Sorry.

—Don't think about it.

—Right.
—Shit.
—I know.

*

—What is it, buddy?
—If you've got 68 balls and you can put them 8 at a time into baskets how many baskets will you need for all 68?
—Um, what. How many balls?
—68.
—Well, how many times does 8 go into 68?
—I know. But it's 8, so does the teacher want 8 baskets with 4 balls outside the baskets, or does she want 9 baskets with one basket with only 4 balls, half full?
—Oh. Well, figuring out the ways of teachers is not my strong suit. What does the teacher want? Hm, a higher salary probably. More respect from the administration.
—*Dad.*
—Sorry. I'd say, mm, 8 and a half baskets.
—A half basket.
—Well.
—That sounds a little lame. Who has a half basket?
—You're right. Say 9 baskets.
—Ok.

—How you doing in math?

—Ok. It's not my best subject.

—It never was mine either.

—I mean, I'm never gonna use it.

—An age-old complaint, I'm afraid, buddy.

—Do you use math?

—Daily. But don't count me, so to speak. You don't want to work retail.

—Maybe I do. Maybe I want to work in a bookstore like you.

—Really?

—Sure.

—I thought you wanted to be a cartoonist.

—Mom said I could be two things. Or more.

—Your mother's a wise woman. Yes. Of course, you can be as many things as you want.

—Really?

—Sure.

—A cartooning bookstore manager.

—Sure.

*

—Book Shoppe.

—

—Oh, hi.

—

—Yes. I mean, well.

—

—It's, you know, difficult.

—

—Yes. I know.

—

—Well.

—

—I don't think so. No.

—

—I just can't, you know. I feel so damn bad.

—

—I know.

—

—It's just, you know. I can't.

—

—I know. I'm sorry.

—

—Yes. I'm sorry.

*

—I wanted to make myself something new. What could that be?

—A VCR repairman? The guy who, you know, gets to wear the little headphones and guide the jumbo jets in on the tarmac?

—Funny. You're a funny funny wife. No, something new to eat. I'm tired of my lunch choices.

—I don't know. I couldn't possibly know.

—It's that between season thing, you know. It's getting warmer and I'm tired of soups, which have seen me through the winter of my discontent, but I'm not quite ready for my summer foods, yet. It's just not time for the cottage cheese dip thing yet, or Aunt Helen's cold rice salad. I hate these between times.

—Just go out at lunch.

—Right. That means the expensive buffet across the street which normally gives me the runs or at least heartburn. Or the chemically retted burgers at McDeath.

—Those aren't your only choices and you know it. I'm finished with this conversation. As of right now I am not talking about your lunches anymore.

—Maybe egg and olive salad.

—Don't use the Easter eggs.

—I thought you had ruled yourself out of the decision-making loop.

—Why did you address me then?

—Well, ok, why not the Easter eggs? They seem the obvious choices for egg salad seeing as how if I use the others I'm gonna have to cook them to the desired turgidity which the Easter eggs already exist at.

—Last year you ate the Easter eggs and got food poisoning.

—Oh yeah.

—Right.

—Maybe tuna.

—

—MAYBE TUNA.

—Jim. Shut up.

—Right. I'm making tuna, he said to himself because there was no one else to care.

—

—And I'm putting a little hardboiled egg in.

*

—Hi.

—Hi to you. Firm resolve.

—I know.

—You gonna make Thursdays your permanent day off?

—Hoo, I better not, ay?

—Come in, please.

—Thanks.

—Sit.

—Thanks. Place looks nice.

—I cleaned.

—Not for me.

—Egoist.

—Right.

—Relax.

—Yes.

—We're in charge, you know.

—Whaddya mean?

—We're in charge of us. We can do or not do anything we want.

—I wish I believed that.

—You know what I mean.

—Yes.

—What I called to tell you yesterday before I was so rudely cut off—

—I'm sorry I—

—I'm kidding. What I called to tell you was I've been thinking and I've come up with a few more compromises. Some alternative plans of my own.

—Hey, that last one worked like a charm.

—Well, in a sense, it did. I mean we touched, which was lovely, but we didn't do anything irreparable, anything soul-damaging.

—We didn't? Reassure me.

—We didn't.

—Ok.

—Ok?

—Maybe we should just pass in the night before, you know, one of us hits the iceberg. Before one of us becomes the fucking iceberg.

—We don't want that. We don't.

—Ok. You're right. Continue. Of course, I'm intrigued by your idea of new compromises. It's very exciting. I mean, it's very exciting that you've been thinking about this.

—About you.

—Yes.

—This is in addition to the very clever ones already outlined. Delightful, as they were. They were *challenging*. Addenda perhaps not called for but desired anyway.

—Indeed.

—Which we haven't even explored yet.

—Gulp.

—Stop saying that. Ok. Katya's Compromise Number One.

—Number four.

—Ok, stickler. Number Four. Dancing, we could dance. Simple, elegant, as sexy as you want.

—One drawback. I'm not Jeff Kutash.

—Who the hell is Jeff Kutash?

—A dancer from TV, from my long ago youth.

—Look, we slow dance, we hold each other, we rub our lower selves against each other. It's not exactly the watusi.

—Hm. Ok. What music?

—Good question. I'm thinking Van Morrison.

—Mm. Uh.

—No good?

—It's, well, he's Dorothea's favorite and we—

—Ok, nuff said. Music is your choice.

—Ok. I'll think about it. What else?

—Strip poker.

—Oo. I like that. I think I remember how to play. How about strip Yahtzee?

—Too deviant. Not exactly time-honored.

—Ok. I really remember how to play poker. I think I'm

pretty good at it.

—From your long ago past, when you were a riverboat gambler?

—Yes. Strip poker. Sounds pretty good.

—Ok. Want to play? I mean, I don't even have to continue I got such an enthusiastic response to that one.

—No, no. Tell me number, um, six. I have to say this is very exciting.

—Guilt levels low?

—Well.

—Ok. Number, as you will have it, six. Dirty Talk.

—Phone sex.

—Right but in person.

—Hm.

—You like?

—I do. I like dirty talk. No touching, no guilt. That could work. I mean, who's ever been hurt by talk?

—Right.

—Hoo. Now what?

—Your choice.

—Really. Let's see, what was left from last time?

—Um, kissing, necking that is and, well—

—Oh yes. Well, let's table that one for now.

—Ok.

—I think...Poker.

—Right.

—You got cards?

—Right here.

—New deck.

—Well. I'm a little embarrassed.

—You devil you. Classic. Bicycle.

—Yes. Only the best for you. You wanna deal?

—Sure.

—You're a pretty good shuffler. You're not like a card shark or anything are you?

—It's sharp, isn't it?

—Is it? I thought it was shark.

—Well, anyway. Yes, I'm a card whatever and I'm gonna strip you naked and leave you humiliated and clothesless.

—Sounds like fun.

—Ok. I deal out five each and then here's the, what, kitty.

—Oh, yeah. You're a gambler all right.

—Ok.

—Um, I want, um, two cards.

—Two.

—Ok.

—And I want three. One, two, three.

—Now what?

—You show me what you've got.

—I thought we were gonna play poker first.

—Ha ha.

—Two twos.

—Very tough. I got nothing.

—Ha. I win. I win.

—Yes.

—Take your clothes off.

—Funny. Here. Here's one shoe.

*

—That's three in a row.

—I know.

—You're no card shark.

—I know.

—Take it off. Take off your pants.

—Alright.

—Nice briefs. Combo boxer/briefs. I like.

—Thank you.

—One more hand and—

—I know, I know.

—Oh boy.

—Look, I've won once. I got your shirt.

—I just didn't have shoes on or you'd be clothesless alone, buddy.

—Right, why didn't you wear shoes?

—Hey, I didn't totally think this out. Besides I knew I could win.

—Ha. I'm a little cold and embarrassed here.

—Embarrassed at losing or at being virtually naked?

—Um, the naked one. I've got a bit of a paunch here.

—Mm. You look yummy. Really.

—Ok. Deal.

—Ok. Five and five and whaddya got?

—Shit.

—Ha ha.

—Gimme three. Shit.

—Ha ha. Two for me. Ok. Show. And I do mean show.

—Nothing. Jack high. I've got nothing jack high.

—Hoo hoo. Three tens. Hoo hoo. Lose them big boy.

—Wait.

—No wait. Lose the briefs. I won fair and square.

—Lemme just—

—What?

—I don't know.

—Ok. Lose them.

—I'll be naked.

—Yes.

—And I'll be naked and you'll be sitting there in jeans and a bra.

—Right. That's the game, bucko.

—Um.

—Stand up and lose them.

—I won't stand. There.

—You're naked.

—Thanks.

—Hoo. I won.

—Yes.

—Ok.

—Now what?

—Lemme just get an eyeful here.

—Please.

—Relax. Lie back and relax.

—I don't know.

—You want me to take my bra off at least. No concession, mind you. I won.

—Right. No, no.

—Come here. Lemme hold you.

—Mm.

—There. You have a nice body.

—No.

—Yes. Your once shriveled manhood is coming to life.

—Mm.

—Nice.

—I.

—Ok.

—It's just.

—Ok. It's all ok. Thanks for the show. Lemme just look a few moments more. Hm.

—Ok.

—Turn around. Nice. Nice ass.

—Well, thanks.

—You're, um—

—Yes.

—Very erect.

—I.

—Ok. Get dressed.

*

—What are you doing?

—I was going to turn the TV off.

—I'm watching the game.

—No, you were in the other room.

—I know but I'm coming back in here now to watch the game.

—Who's winning?

—I see what you're saying but you're out of your element here. You don't watch sports. You don't know how it's done.

—Clear me up.

—Well, what you don't understand about watching sports on TV is you can tune in and tune out. You know one of my favorite activities in the world is to have a game on with the sound off and a good book in my lap. That's luxury, that's life at its best.

—Jim, you were in the other room playing a game with Connie.

—No, I was showing him how to set something up. I was gone ten, fifteen minutes.

—Ok.

—It's not like a movie where you're gonna miss major plot elements if you don't pay close attention. That's sports. It exists in the moment, I mean, this is happening right now, somewhere far, far away—

—Cleveland.

—Ok.

—That's not that far away.

—And I'm here, partaking of it, experiencing it. It is coloring my world and I am part of it and it is part of me but—

—Go on.

—I lost my thread.

—You've lost it all right.

—Ok, anyway. Can I leave the TV on?

*

—Hot enough for you?

—What a hackneyed conversational opener. I expect more from you.

—Ok, Marco. Don't you hate Memphians who are constantly going on about the heat. It's Memphis, for Chrisake. Move to St. Paul.

—Move to Winnipeg.

—Move to Sioux Falls.

—Sioux Falls cold?

—Who knows?

—Yeah, who knows Sioux Falls?

—Makes you want to invent new ways to talk about it. Wanna fit in, you know. Want to connect with my contemporaries, no longer want to be the odd man out, the outsider, the rebel. Want to employ colorful representations of our common state.

—What the hell are you talking about?

—Ask me if it's hot enough for me?

—Ffft.

—Ask me.

—Jimbo, hot enough, etc.?

—I feel like I'm walking through God's urinary tract.

—Ha ha. Good one.

—Serves the purpose.

—Yeah, that'll connect you to the common man.

—Well.

—You need those, though, those comebacks to vacuous conversational gambits.

—Sure.

*

—You ever met the little blonde works with Mark? Kathy or something.

—Yeah. You know I have. We've been in the shop together.

—Oh. Right.

—What about her?

—Mark said something about her, that she looks like Allie McBeal or something.

—Yeah, she does sort of.

—Yeah. She's cute, I guess.

—If you don't mind we can talk about her later. I'm naked here and hoping for something more than talk about some other woman.

—Oh. Right. Sorry.

—Thank you.

—You are naked.

—Under these covers, yes.

—Wow. Look at that.

—Thank you.

—Let me just go down here doing some exploring. Some spelunking.

—Mm hm.

—Oh, look.

—Mmm.

—Mmff hursss flll.

—I can't hear you but don't stop.

—

—Oh, don't stop.

—Mm.

—Mm hm, mm hm.

—Oo, you're wet. You are ready.

—Yes.

—Diaphragm in?

—Just fuck me.

—Mm hm.

—Oh, just fuck me.

—Mm.

—Fuck me, fuck me, and fuck me.

*

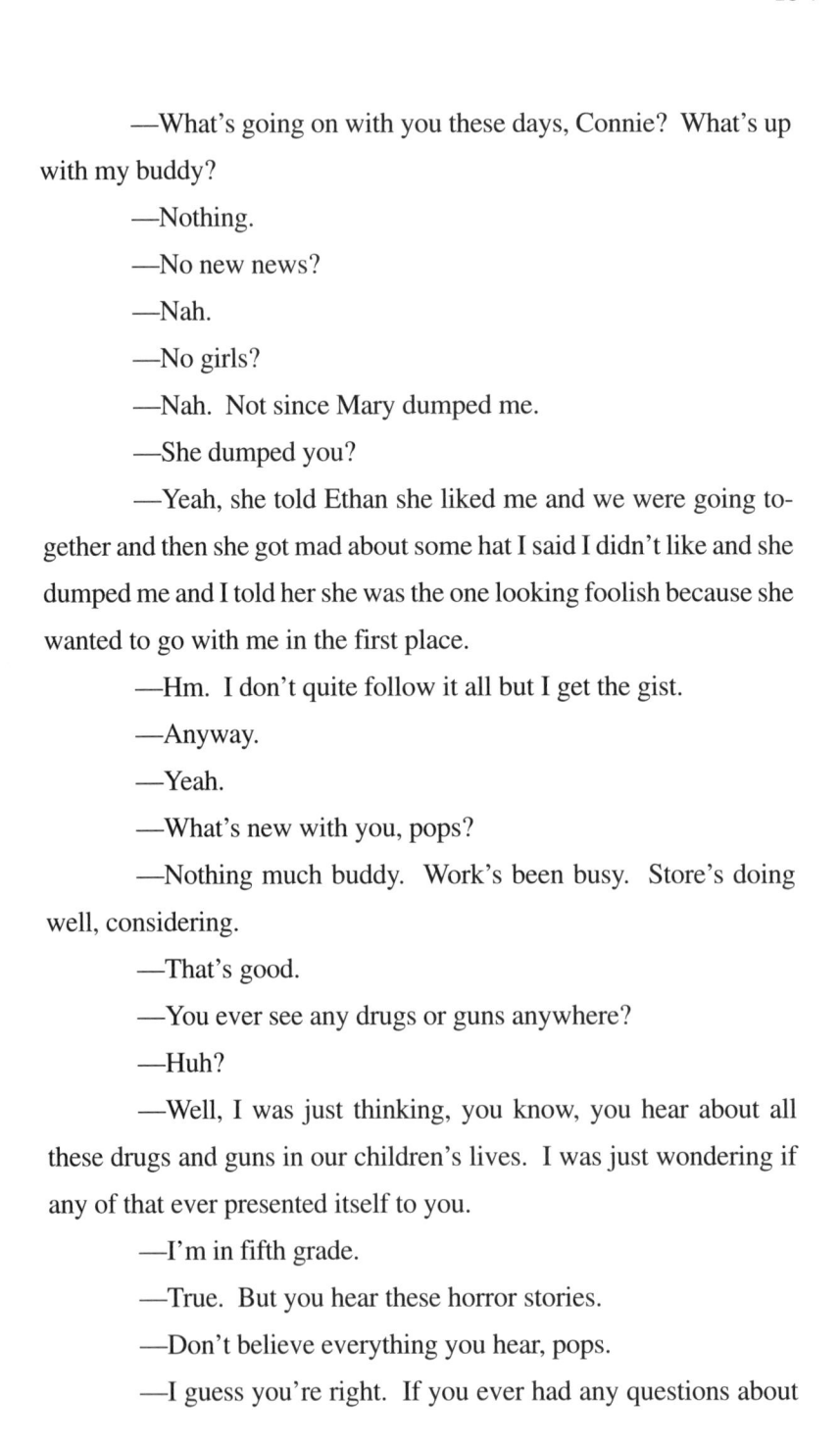

—What's going on with you these days, Connie? What's up with my buddy?

—Nothing.

—No new news?

—Nah.

—No girls?

—Nah. Not since Mary dumped me.

—She dumped you?

—Yeah, she told Ethan she liked me and we were going together and then she got mad about some hat I said I didn't like and she dumped me and I told her she was the one looking foolish because she wanted to go with me in the first place.

—Hm. I don't quite follow it all but I get the gist.

—Anyway.

—Yeah.

—What's new with you, pops?

—Nothing much buddy. Work's been busy. Store's doing well, considering.

—That's good.

—You ever see any drugs or guns anywhere?

—Huh?

—Well, I was just thinking, you know, you hear about all these drugs and guns in our children's lives. I was just wondering if any of that ever presented itself to you.

—I'm in fifth grade.

—True. But you hear these horror stories.

—Don't believe everything you hear, pops.

—I guess you're right. If you ever had any questions about

anything, you'd come to me, right? Drugs, sex, anything.

—Sure.

—Really, now. No secrets.

—Sure, Dad.

*

—What are you reading?

—Mm. I don't know. A couple of things. I'm having trouble staying with anything. I get antsy, I get agitated, I want too much. Is this symptomatic of some decrepitude in me or are the novels today just not that compelling?

—Hm. Both, maybe.

—Anyway, I'm reading the new David Plante and the new Alice Walker.

—The last time I read two books at once—

—Don't say it.

—I thought Emma Bovary was captured by the Morlocks.

—I believe you've used that joke before.

—Yes.

—So, what are you reading, he asks like he is supposed to.

—Meaning?

—Meaning you asked me so I would ask you.

—Oh. Probably. Forget it.

—Oh come on, don't be so sensitive.

—Nah, it's not important.

—C'mon. I'm dying to know what you're reading.

—Nah. I can't even remember.

—Right.

—You wanna go someplace tonight? You want to go to the movies or something instead of just sitting here, nursing our respective libations?

—Really. What a wild idea. You are a wild man.

—Yes.

—You really want to go out.

—Sure. Got a good mix of medications in me, feeling somewhat gregarious.

—What you want to see?

—I don't know. Nothing any good ever plays here anymore.

—That's encouraging. Yeah, let's run right out and see something mediocre.

—Well.

—How about *Saving Private Ryan*?

—You're kidding, right? You're kidding.

—Sort of.

—Don't get me started on Steven Spielberg.

—Right.

—I don't know. You want to go poke around the second-hand record stores.

—CD.

—Yeah. I can't say CD stores, though. It just sounds wrong. Like people who say, the new disk by, as in "Have you heard the new disk by The Knack?"

—Right.

—Sounds phony or something.

—It does.

—The new album by. Still sounds better.

—Yes.

—If not technically correct.

—Right.

—I don't know. There's not much I wanna buy. Even if I had the money.

—Ok.

—You wanna do some best movies with?

—Sure.

—Um. You start.

—Uh, Peter O'Toole.

—By the way, I'm reading *Midnight's Children*.

—Oh.

—Aren't you gonna ask me how it is?

—Sure. How is it?

—Forget it.

*

—I am drawn by the gentle drift of your surface, a gravity as serious as flowers, as final as the dark corner of everywhere. Someone else may handle the world's snakes. I bloom and uncover in the lamplight of your bedside and the wavelike slap of our overlapping draws silence like blood. There is stillness and rest in your forehead, an ocean of contentment in your mouth full of voice. We talk for hours until sunlight. Nothing happens save the world changing, swiftly, begrudgingly, for good.

*

—Hello.

—

—What's wrong? You look ... ashen. Come in.

—

—Are you crying? Did something happen? Jim, Chrissakes, talk to me.

—Nothing. Happened.

—Well, what is it. Come here. Sit down.

—I can't be here.

—Ok. Sit. Be still for a minute.

—

—Here. Just hold me. Let me get my arms around you. Nothing's wrong, nothing's happening. Just be still. Let me hold you.

—

—Here. Right here.

—

—Be still. Shh.

—

—That's it. Just hold me. Just.
—Yes.
—Hold me.
—Yes.
—There.
—I can't be here.
—Ok. It's ok.
—I.
—Shh. Shh.
—
—There.
—I gotta go.

*

—Hey. Where you been?
—I was in Katey's room, folding clothes. What are you doing?
—Game's fixing to come on.
—Who's playing, she asked as if she cared.
—Um, Celtics and—
—Yes?
—Somebody.
—Important game.
—Well, it is. It will figure in the playoff picture.

—Okay.

—You finished with the clothes?

—Yep. I was thinking about going out to the consignment shop. Ok if the kids stay here with you?

—Um. Sure.

—What? You want me to take Katey?

—Um.

—You gonna do something besides watch the game?

—Well, no. It's ok. Katey can stay with me.

—If she's gonna bother you.

—She's just in that chattering phase. She can talk a blue streak and she expects you to actually answer. I mean, it's not just rhetorical. When she asks you something she wants an answer. A germane answer.

—And?

—It's ok. I'll watch her. I just wanted to watch this is all. She's so distracting.

—You can't do both?

—Sure. But you know, to catch the whole, you know, flow of the game you kinda have to pay attention.

—You do.

—Well, yeah. A basketball game is like a novel, there's a flow, a plot. You wouldn't understand.

—Ok. I'll take Katey.

—No, no. Where's Connie?

—In his room, I think.

—He's not. I was just in there. Did he go down to Ethan's?

—Um. I think he did.

—Is it possible to lose a whole ten-year-old boy?

—No. Yes. He's at Ethan's.
—Ok.

*

—So.

—So. You have a new plan?

—No. No, not really. I am weak. I was hoping to fall back on some of the already established plans.

—Uh huh. Jim. Is this eating you up? Is this a good idea at all? I mean, we are avoiding an affair, but just barely. Just technically.

—No, I'm ok. I mean, my guilt is minimal. We haven't done anything yet.

—Yet. Ok, so you've told Dorothea about our aborted massage, our aborted strip poker.

—Of course not.

—Ok.

—I'm sorry. I should go.

—Oh, stop. I want to compromise on this as much as you do. I like you, I really do. I want to spend some time with you however crazy this is. I want these goofy middle grounds. I do.

—You're wonderful, Katya. You're special.

—Sure.

—So.

—Again, so? Which game do we play today?

—I don't know. Maybe I should go.

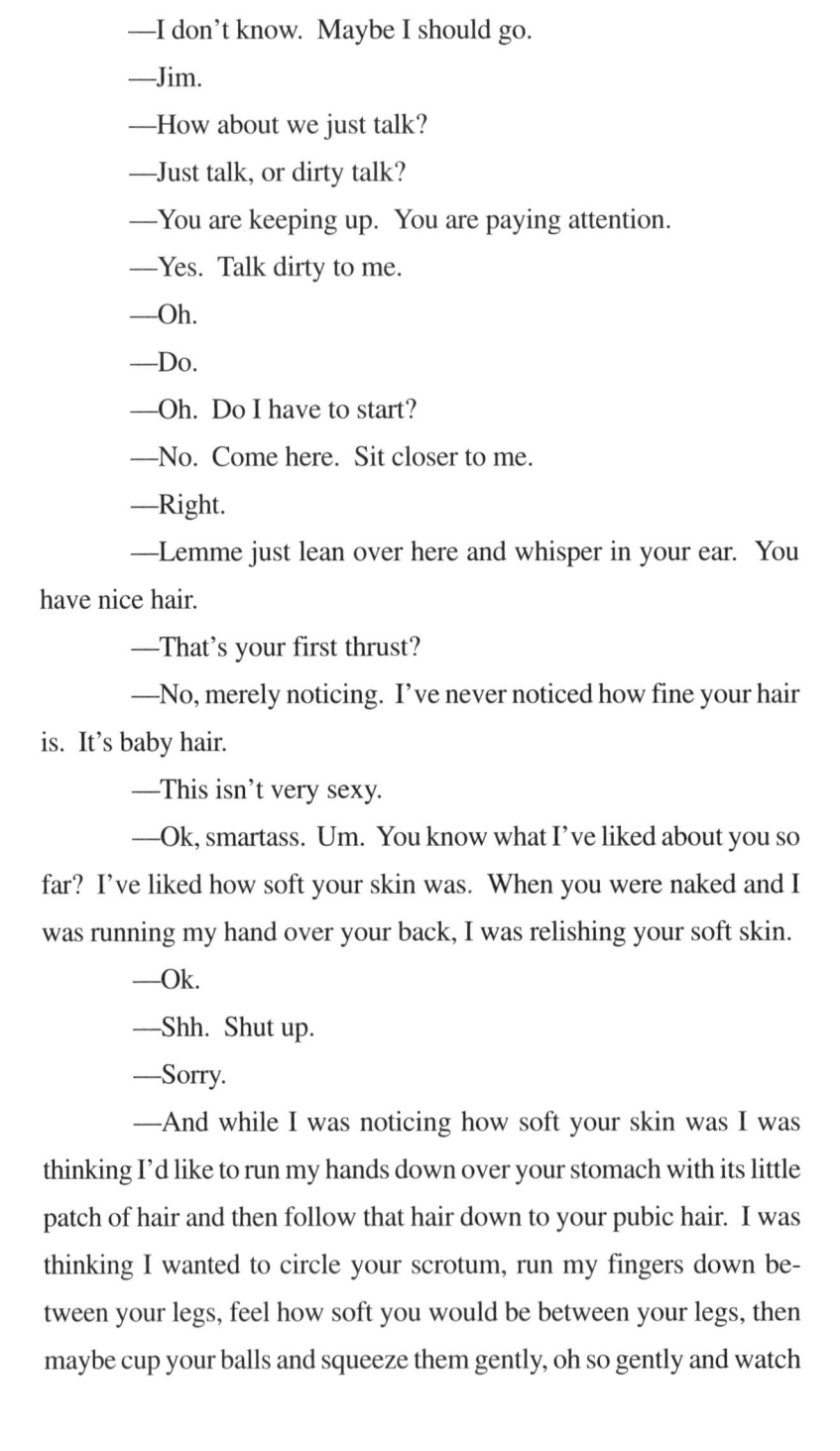

—Jim.

—How about we just talk?

—Just talk, or dirty talk?

—You are keeping up. You are paying attention.

—Yes. Talk dirty to me.

—Oh.

—Do.

—Oh. Do I have to start?

—No. Come here. Sit closer to me.

—Right.

—Lemme just lean over here and whisper in your ear. You have nice hair.

—That's your first thrust?

—No, merely noticing. I've never noticed how fine your hair is. It's baby hair.

—This isn't very sexy.

—Ok, smartass. Um. You know what I've liked about you so far? I've liked how soft your skin was. When you were naked and I was running my hand over your back, I was relishing your soft skin.

—Ok.

—Shh. Shut up.

—Sorry.

—And while I was noticing how soft your skin was I was thinking I'd like to run my hands down over your stomach with its little patch of hair and then follow that hair down to your pubic hair. I was thinking I wanted to circle your scrotum, run my fingers down between your legs, feel how soft you would be between your legs, then maybe cup your balls and squeeze them gently, oh so gently and watch your prick rise up. Oo, I saw your erect prick, didn't I? Didn't I want it then? I wanted to run my hands over it, it looked so eager, so tight. I wanted to pump it a bit and hear your moans. I wanted to watch it engorge and squeeze its perfect little head and run my fingers over it and over your balls and drive you crazy with the mm pressure on your erect prick. And then, slowly I wanted to lower my mouth toward you, mm coming closer and closer, my tongue extended, closer to your straining prick. And then, quickly, unexpectedly, plunge my wet mouth over you and suck and suck and suck and pull on you until you exploded into my mouth.

—Nn.

—How was that?

—Painful.

—Oh?

—You're incredibly good at that. I'm so hard right now.

—Let's see.

—No.

—Move your hands. Oh, my. That is a bulge.

—Yes.

—Now do me.

—Um.

—Come on. Before your excitement dies.

—Lean over you and talk in your ear?

—If you'd like.

—Ok. C'mere. Um. Let's see. When I was rubbing you, that first time. Is it okay if I use the same format you established?

—Yes, yes. Just arouse me.

—So, when I was massaging you and your skin was so smooth. Um, I was looking at your perfect ass in those sheer little panties, oh why were those panties so brief, I was looking at the shadowy shape of you through that material. I could see your dark crack and then when I pulled them down partway there was your beautiful ass. It was like it was shining there, so round and soft. I wanted to put my lips on it and run my tongue around it. I wanted to slide my tongue into your crack and lick it up and down.

—Oh. I'm squirming.

—Shh. And lick up and down and poke my tongue gently into your anus, quick like a snake, in and out, and then lift your buttocks gently and push my tongue between your legs and feel the curve of your cheeks against my face and eat you savagely, putting my tongue into you, pushing my face up against you, sucking on your clit. Um, and while I was eating you I wanted you to position yourself over me and pull my pants open and pull my erect cock out into the air and shove it into your mouth as if you couldn't do without it, sucking it and—

—What? Why did you stop?

—I realized I was having you do me in my fantasy.

—That's ok.

—Kind of selfish. Let me get back to doing you.

—I, I think I'm aroused enough here.

—Really. This was pretty good. This wasn't as dangerous. I'm, I'm feeling all right about this.

—Good. I'm horny as hell.

—Well. Me, too. But at least there was no touching, little guilt, I think.

—Kiss me.

—Well. C'mere.

—Mmm.

—Mm.

—You're still erect.

—Yes.

—Mmm. Feels good. Let me put my cheek against it. Mmm.

—Oh. Uh, oh.

—Sorry.

—That's ok. It's not like I don't want you to.

—I know.

—Well.

—Well. Kiss me again.

*

—Ask me what the number one rule of comedy is.

—Hey, Jimbo, what's the number one rule of com—

—Timing.

—Ha. That's funny.

—Don't you hate it when someone says, "That's funny," instead of actually laughing. Or, like, "You're *bad,*" in response to some perfectly placed aperçu.

—I meant it.

—I know you did. Here's a question for you. Is it still funny if someone doesn't get it?

—Whaddya mean?

—Does a joke have to make the connection for it to be funny, for it to be genuinely humorous?

—Like the tree in the forest thing. This is Zen, right?

—Right. I mean, the other day, I was mock-singing to Dorothea, softshoeing around the kitchen getting dinner ready, scat-singing that song, you know, rock chick with the great legs—

—Sheryl Crow.

—Very good. Right. And I was singing, "As the sun comes up over Corbett Monica Boulevard."

—Who's Corbett Monica?

—Jesus. You said the same thing. I thought we were the same age, had the same pop artifacts for touchstones. I thought you'd get it.

—Take a deep breath. I do get it. I was anticipating what Dorothea said.

—Oh. And you hit it right on the nose.

—Right.

—Ok.

—You're *bad*.

*

—Hello?

—

—Hi, Ma.

—

—Yes. Yes, everyone's fine.

—

—Oh, I'm sorry. Everyone's fine, ma. I'm sorry you had an unpleasant dream.

—

—Yes.

—

—I am, ma. I'm sorry. We're fine. Stop worrying.

—

—Yes. How's Dad?

—

—I know he can be grouchy. Yes.

—

—Well, Ma. You've managed 51 years. I would have thought you had figured out how to live with him.

—

—I know. But he's also very sweet.

—

—He is. He is too sweet, Ma.

—

—Ok. I gotta go here, Ma. Katey's trying to go potty for the first time by herself.

—

—She's out somewhere.

—

—No, I know where she is, it's just not that important.

—

—Ok, Target. She went to Target to get tampons.

—

—I didn't mean to be rude, Ma, but I gotta go here. Katey's in the bathroom by herself.

—

—Yes, she is getting big. She thinks she's sixteen, she thinks she rules the roost. Yesterday she told me to stop singing because she was trying to watch TV. I tell you the mouth on her and only three.

—

—Yes. Yes, I better.

—

—Ok, Ma. Love you too.

*

—Hello. Looking for anything in particular?

—Don't think so.

—Ok.

—Fiction?

—Right here. Alphabetical by author. Tricky South Americans by middle moniker or whatever they call it.

—Pardon?

—Garcia Marquez under G, that sort of thing.

—I see.

—You look familiar.

—I come in here. Zuzu Barnes.

—Jim. Zuzu, huh?

—My father. Jimmy Stewart fan.

—Uh huh. Well, it's lovely.

—Thanks. You ever heard of Henry Green?

—My heart just stopped.

—Pardon?

—No one asks for Henry Green. Here. I'm trying not to act over-excited, like we never sell any literary fiction. Ok. Let's see what—here, we've only got second hand, of course—he can't stay in print, poor sap. But that's a nice Viking copy of *Party Going* and this *Loving* is a steal at 10.

—Sounds like you're familiar with him.

—Oh, yes. Love those Brits. Twentieth century Brits, that's my passion, I guess.

—I'm impressed.

—Don't be. Books, *c'est moi*. They're all I know. Don't ask me who the Secretary of State is or the capital of Montana or where the Apennines are, or even what the Apennines are. Or, say, how to change a spark plug wire, if spark plugs have wires and they occasionally need changing.

—Ok. So you're pretty much useless outside the bookstore.

—Pretty much.

—Are you always this charming to your customers?

—No. And this is about it. I just maxed out, charmwise. I just hit empty.

—Why did I rate the full tank?

—Pretty woman wanting Henry Green.

—Ah. Thank you.

—Could have been cute and buxom looking for *The Dream Songs*.

—Uh huh.

—Or a combo of Heather Graham eyes and Yeats.

—Nice butt and Anthony Burgess.

—Very good.

—I get it.

—Ok then.

—You're a flirt.

—As are you.

—I suppose so. You wanna go for coffee?

—Flattered like I haven't been in ages but, see, ring here. Married.

—Figures.

—Enjoyed talking anyway. Hope you'll come back.

—Yes. Me, too.

—Zuzu.

—Yes?

—It's fun to say.

—I know. Knock yourself out.

—Zuzu. You want a Henry Green then?

—Think I'll try a little *Loving*.

—Ah.

*

—Hi, Sweet.

—Peter Pan's not mean.

—No?

—He's not mean. He's nice.

—Uh huh. Just a bit of a rascal.

—

—Is that Peter Pan you've got there?

—Has he got a feather in his hat?

—Looks like.

—He's not mean.

—Nope.

—Captain Hook's not very nice. He's not very nice.

—I know. He's not.

—He's mean to Peter.

—He sure is.

—Peter Pan's not mean.

—Ok.

—He's a girl.

—Oh.

*

—Do you think The Monkees were only a cheap, knock-off Beatles, or do you think they emerged as real talents, with a flair for pop hooks and a genuine rock and roll sensibility?

—Gee, Jim. I don't know. *There's* some real meat to tug

around.

—All right. What do you want to talk about?

—I don't know.

—We sound like the vultures in *Jungle Book*.

—Who were cheap, knock-off Beatles.

—Ha. Yes.

—Kids alright?

—Sure, sure. Connie's doing alright. He's got some blues in him formerly unforeseen. I guess that goes with hidden depths. You gotta take the dark with the light.

—Yeah. You wouldn't want him shallow.

—Shallow and happy, I don't know. Which would be better? A little less introspection and a little more unexamined lightness.

—It's not like Connie's morose. He seems to have a real light touch to things.

—Yeah, you're right. He's ok. Just, you know, when he seems sad and I ask him what's wrong and he says, nothing, in that way that might mean, please help me figure this out and might mean please leave me alone, I don't know. That's a tough call. I feel worthless just letting it go by, you know, just accepting that, "nothing," and continuing on. Am I ignoring an area that needs exploring?

—I've never known you to ignore an area that needs exploring. I think hands off might be the best thing here, you know? Let it ride unless it surfaces again.

—Yeah.

—What do I know?

—No, you're a big help. Always.

—And, the little one. How's she?

—Oh, great. Full of the business.

—Ha. That's your princess.

—Yes, it is. She's a wonder, she is. How bout you? Ginger okay? Everything hunky-dory on the homefront?

—Sure, sure. Same.

—Same as in boring and no-thrills, or same as in, it sure is good to have a mate and some stability?

—Jesus, I don't know. You know. She's wonderful.

—She is.

—I love her.

—No question.

—And the sex, you know, it's still pretty good.

—You sound doubtful.

—I guess I am, a little.

—Didn't go for the porno movie, fantasy-driven, all-out sexfest you had in mind?

—Something like that.

—You suggested a porno movie.

—I went out and got one.

—Without asking her.

—Yeah.

—And she freaked.

—No. Not exactly. She was, how shall we say, dubious.

—But you watched it together?

—Yeah. She, I don't know, I couldn't tell whether she was interested or not. She watched with this passive mask, as if she were watching an ad for used cars. I mean, there were these two athletes with their privacies hung out there for all the world to see, their faces in each other's crotches, and she just sat there.

—Did you then have sex, if I'm not prying, detailwise?

—Yeah.

—And was it hotter than usual?

—Um. Sort of. I guess.

—Well, then, I'd say she was paying attention. You know, she absorbed the stimuli and responded in her fashion.

—Yeah. I guess.

—Well.

—She did this weird thing.

—Oh, boy.

—No, I mean nothing newly imaginative. She's not, what?, experimental. But in the course of things, I think she had me in her firm grip, and she said, sort of *sotto voce*, "He sure had a big one."

—Really. Meaning the guy in the movie?

—Yeah.

—Wistfully? Longingly?

—No. I don't know. Not like she was wishing mine were like his, at least I don't think so, but more like she was considering the male organ for the first time.

—Was it? A big one?

—He had quite a hose on him.

—Hm. Could pay off in the long run.

—What do you mean?

—Don't take offense. I just mean, you never know when you've opened a door, a window of opportunity. Ginger may be thinking of male organs now, pondering them, and, later, subtly, this may add to your pleasure and hers, your pleasure together. Know what I mean?

—I guess so. You've got some funny ideas. You, maybe, think about this too much.

—Maybe. The unexamined sex life is not worth having.

—Hm. I might disagree. Too much thinking can ruin it.

—I might agree.

—You're a funny bird.

—Yes. Yes, I am.

—You haven't seen Katya again have you?

—Smooth segue. No.

—Good.

—Yes.

—Shit.

—I know.

—I thought—

—No lectures, please.

—Are you not happy with Dorothea? Is it not everything you wanted?

—Yes. I am. It is. She is. She hangs colored lights around our house, strings of small paper lanterns. I mean, she's—festive. She's a carnival. It's, no two ways about it, a high quality life.

—And, yet—

—Yes, and yet. Consider the human animal.

—You're letting yourself off a little easily, aren't you? Forgiving yourself by writing it off to warped human nature?

—No. Believe me I don't let myself off easily. Ever.

—I know.

—She's so—

—Don't.

—Ok.

—Well.

—So soft.

—Stop.

*

—Are you cooking tonight?

—And how.

—Jim, are you making dinner?

—Sure. I can. I didn't thaw anything. You want that tomato, rice, beans thing?

—Sure.

—You don't seem enthusiastic.

—No. That would be good. What would we give the kids?

—I don't know, the usual. Connie eats only pasta and dairy. Katey only fruit and yogurt. What else can we give them?

—Pizza.

—I can do that. I can cook a frozen pizza for them.

—I was thinking delivery.

—Just for them.

—No, for everybody.

—Why didn't you just say that?

—I don't know. I didn't think you wanted pizza.

—I can always eat pizza.

—Can we afford it?

—Sure. You got any money in your checking account?

—As usual, no.

—That's ok, I do.

—You sure?

—Yeah.

—Where are the kids?

—Connie's in his room, slaughtering aliens and Katey, let's see. I think she's out back.

—By herself?

—Is that bad? Fly's back there.

—While very smart, I don't think the dog is a great sitter.

—No a herder.

—Very funny. Do you really think she's alright back there?

—Sure. I'll go check on her.

—I'll order.

—Ok.

—You want anything special?

—Pepperoni.

—Men.

—What?

—Men eat pepperoni. That's all.

—And women vegetables.

—Exactly.

—It's certain that fine women eat vegetable pizza with their meat.

—Right.

—Crazy vegetable pizza.

—Don't try to refine it. It was funny enough.

—Hey, who made you joke judge?

—This marriage did, sweetheart.

—Ha. Right.

—I love you.
—And I you.

*

—You ever feel like it's all written down already and we're just playing it out?
—I'm not following you.
—Like, you know, I have to keep reminding myself that any event I'm anticipating or dreading or looking forward to has not happened yet and is entirely flexible, anything may transpire. Sometimes I feel powerless and unable to effect anything, change anything. I have to remind myself, that, say, if I'm alone with Katey for an afternoon that I am in control of the situation and I can decide whether we, I don't know, get down on the floor and do a puzzle or whether she just goes in Connie's room and watches a video. It's like I can foresee the afternoon and she's in another room and I'm alone with my thoughts or my book or a game on the TV and that's just the way it's gonna be. I'm not a factor, somehow.
—Hm. That's freakish. I guess I see what you mean.
—Like sometimes when I'm watching a basketball game, say, and I have to consciously think: this is happening right now, anyone can win, it will be decided as I watch it, it is not predestined. The Kings may upset the Knicks. Penny Hardaway *may* have a good game

or a mediocre game or a dominating game. It isn't preset. I don't know. It's like I'm living my life by rote.

—You feel like an actor.

—I don't know. That sounds so existential, so phony drama like. Did we read too much Sartre and Kafka and Camus when we were impressionable youths?

—If you call twenties youth.

—Yeah. Is that what's wrong with us?

—Could be. It's like when I'm leaving a record store that has those security gates and I know I haven't stolen anything but I have this moment of existential terror that that thing's gonna go off and my whole life is gonna be changed. I'm gonna be revealed as the criminal that I am. That's Kafka.

—Maybe it's just that Kafka had it right. He just understood.

—Yeah.

—That guilt. Yeah, that's modern man, guilt. Guilt in Levi's.

—Ha, right.

—Of course, we have things to be guilty about. It's not like it's imaginary.

—Right.

—Some of us more than others.

—Ok.

*

—Katey, the world is not kind to imagination. You must see it clearly. If I've cleared a space where kindness rules, and the incipient snake is as just as the loving rhinoceros, I am sorry. Your crystal eyes refract. I want that kind of wonder. And if I've seen too much and listen for the owl like a quivering field mouse I need only your babble to make it right again. The world will not conform. No, the serpents always rule, the beasts will be rewarded for utter beastliness. But we can still read the story of the monkey who uses balloons to see the city, and the animals whose democracy is untainted, and we can see ourselves through their eyes. Vagabond humans with no more idea how to run a planet than a household, but in our pockets we have magic seeds and here under our kindly surfaces a pulse still radical with imagination. We can still hope and sometimes, by mere hoping, we can make it happen. Voila, a life.

*

—Well.
—What's the prescription for today, doctor?
—You wanna play doctor?
—Sure.
—You're always game.
—I am. It's one of my qualities.
—You're very sweet.
—Thank you.

—I've been thinking about you. Too much.

—That is the danger, isn't it. Invasion from within.

—Is it called invasion if it's from within?

—I don't know.

—Inversion?

—I don't know.

—Anyway, you're wonderful.

—Again, thank you. You want to just talk. We never, actually, just talk. I guess there's a million things we don't know about each other. Maybe that's bad. Does it seem like all we do is lubricate each other's parts, that we haven't spent any time whatsoever getting to know each other, I mean, you know, intellectually. Is this bad? Is this perverse? Sick, somehow?

—I don't know.

—You wanna just talk?

—No. I've had it up to here with talk. I spend entirely too much of my life talking. And I'm a bad talker, too.

—How so?

—Egotistical. Only really interested in talking about me, not really listening to what others say, not really tuning in.

—Hm. You don't seem quite so self-centered to me.

—What?

—Very funny.

—No, I mean. I don't want to talk. That sounds horrible. I do want to know you. In other ways. I do. I just, I'm just feeling kind of intellectually spent. Does that seem fair? No, of course not. Can we just sit here, maybe silently holding hands. Maybe just hold each other.

—Sure. That was a lot of talk actually. I feel like I know you better already.

—Uh oh.

—Right.

—So. Here. Here's my hand.

—Thank you. You have very slim hands, girl-like. Sylph hands.

—You're talking too much.

—I am.

—Here.

—Yes.

—

—

—This is nice, actually.

—Shh.

—Sorry.

—

—

—Mmm.

—So, Doctor, what do you think is wrong with me?

—Well.

—Could it be logorrhea?

—I don't know. We better have a thorough examination. Take off your clothes.

—Yes, Doctor.

—That's a good patient.

—Mm, hm.

—Now, let's see. Let's have a look at that vaginal region.

—Oh, Doctor.

—Please, Miss. I'm a professional. Just open your legs a

little wider.

—Mmmmm.

*

—How's it going with Ginger?

—Fine. As always.

—Right.

—Meaning.

—Nothing. Are you defensive?

—Sorry.

—Ok. Sex good?

—Yes. Sure.

—Good. Anything—

—You know, you might be a little sex obsessed.

—Really?

—A little. You know what Anne Tyler says somewhere, Life is really just a mild R, half sex, half grocery shopping.

—Sounds right to me.

—Sometimes I think you picture it a little harder, maybe a cable-version X.

—Ha, ha. Maybe. But, you know, I mean, it's all around us. Sex. It's everywhere now. In ads, in magazines, the newspaper, even in cartoons, for God's sake. It's been cheapened, devalued. You know, I love sex, I value it. I want it examined, revered, and reinstated in our psyches like before Madison Avenue got a hold of it, before Hollywood did. Tall order I know. But I want it sensual again, gritty again, intimate again. Not this sanitized, slick version movies give us. Not this tool to make us want better cars, beer, vacations. I want it sacred again so that it is the coin of the realm, emotionally speaking, the intimate communication it was meant to be.

—So you have an agenda? There is a purpose to your preoccupation?

—Oh, not so clearly defined as all that. I mean, I'm just a horny little American male, talking about things that titillate me.

—There you go.

—But underneath there is the belief that sex has been turned over to corporatespeak, that it needs to be rehumanized. It *is* life-affirming, at its most basic, at its radix. It literally affirms life. It's also entirely pleasurable.

—Entirely?

—Well maybe that's too strong.

—Alright.

—Don't you agree?

—Sure. You're ranting though.

—I know.

—You're mad.

—I know.

—Alright.

*

—Can I help you?

—I'd like to return this book.

—Ok. What's wrong with it?

—The pages. Look. They're cut crooked.

—Crooked?

—The edges are all rough.

—Um, that's the style, I'm afraid. It's done that way on purpose on certain books. It's supposed to be classy. It's called, I think, uncut pages.

—I don't like it.

—Ok. I can refund—

—I'd like them cut please.

—I'm sure there are many books here either way. If you'd like to—

—No, I'd like that book with smooth edged pages.

—I don't think that's possible, sir.

—Could you search for one for me?

—I could, yes, but I believe this is the way this book was produced. All copies of it are going to have these uncut edges. All.

—I would like to try a search. You do book searches, don't you?

—Yes, sir. I'll give it a try. It's your $2.

—Ok.

—Ok, sir.

—That's all I'm asking.

*

—I tell you what I don't get is these women's magazines—have you seen them, *Elle* and whatever. They're like those hamburgers of our youth, the kind you used to get at little no-name fast food places, that were, you know, 30% soybean filler—and this was before they figured out that soybean filler was better for you than beef. These publications have so little content, so little to say. It's emblematic of our times, maybe. For one thing it takes forever just to get to a table of contents—what is all this photographic overload? —I mean like 96 pages in and here's a list of contributors you'll find *in* the magazine. Where have we been up till now? Some nether region which is neither magazine nor *a-magazine*. Then, really, you flip through it. There are all these very attractive people in black and white photographs, stark, arty, page after page, but I don't know what they mean. They're attractive—the people are damn attractive but I don't know if they're advertising anything except in the large world-conglomerate sense we mean now that asserts that everything is advertising because everything is for sale. But, what, specifically, are these pictures about? Have I been left out? Did I miss a class? It's like trying to pick up on the plotline of Mary Worth by concentrating real hard for a week's worth of strips—you can't do it. It stays just beyond your comprehension. You'll NEVER get it. You're not inside. I mean in *Elle* I see this photo of someone I vaguely admire, Ethan Hawke, say, or, no, there was this photo of the poet David St. John and in small print next to one of his body parts there are these little words, *Mr. St. John's cloth-*

ing by Perry Ellis. Etc. I mean, what shit. What sellout. I hate them. I hate them all. Anyone, anyone in these magazines is going to a special place in hell reserved for the congenitally shallow. This magazine culture is insidious, it's dangerous, and it's destructive.

—Slow down, Jimbo. That's overkill. You don't *hate* them.

—Oh, yes. All of them. The whole magazine population. I obliterate them with my hatred.

*

—I broke another one of the blue glasses again today.

—Damn. We need to get another set. Were you mad again?

—No. I didn't throw it. I just broke it in the dishwasher. I packed them too tight.

—Oh.

—Am I really that much of an ogre? Do I really display an inordinate temper?

—No, honey. I didn't mean to imply.

—Well, Jesus. I don't really think of myself as violent, or extreme in my emotions. Am I deluded?

—No, dear. Don't exaggerate. I didn't mean.

—Sure.

—Really, Jim. C'mere. What did you do today?

—Nothing. Tried to write.

—Did you go out? I called.

—I had the phone unplugged. I was trying to write.
—Oh.
—I'm gonna go now.
—Where?
—Into the study. I don't know.
—You don't know?
—I don't know. Into the kitchen to throw some dishes around.
—Ok.

*

—Marco.
—What else, Jim? Is there anything else as fulfilling, as life-affirming as sex?
—Sure.
—For instance.
—Fathering, for sure. Looking into those crystal blues of Connie's or Katey's is worth any number of orgasms. I'd give them all up for the kids, if it came to that. No contest. Though, jeez, I hope I don't have to.
—Of course.
—Marriage at its best.
—Marriage as an institution?
—Marriage as an agreement between two people, as a con-

struct between two lovers. At its best, marriage produces this table where plans are made, this space. I mean, the best of times with Dorothea is when we lay things out, just little things, tonight we'll go get Connie new shoes. This Saturday we'll look for that Barbie Katey wants. Maybe the zoo, maybe we'll stay home. Maybe this summer we ought to go to Dauphin Island again. Or practical things. How are we gonna dole out our funds this month, how much to the hospital bill, how much to Working Assets. Are we gonna order that set of knives, are we gonna join that CD club online?

—Interesting. I see what you mean. Marriage as a group dynamic, a group of two.

—Or four in my case.

—Yes.

—Very fulfilling.

—Right. Anything else?

—Writing. When I wrote.

—You were good. You just give it up?

—I guess. Lost the faith. But, when it was good, near as I can remember, it felt omnipotent. You know, creating, having the words just come, almost as if unbidden. That was exhilarating. Near as I can remember.

—You ought to try again. Pick it back up. You know what Thurber said, don't get it right, get it written. Just do it, you know. Put some words down, even if they are the wrong words.

—Maybe.

—Could keep you from other diversions.

—Nah. We're not like that. We're not that subdivided, that compartmentalized. One obsession, one inclination does not rule out any other. We're steppenwolfs; we're like endless permutations in a diamond's reflections.

—Sure.

—Sorry. Too fancy.

—No, I'm with you. Just thinking out loud, you know.

—I know.

—You want to go somewhere?

—Where's Dorothea?

—She took the kids to see *Mulan*.

—Oh. Where can we go?

—I don't know. You want to just listen to some music.

—It sounds like we're sixteen again. You want to come over and hear my new Black Sabbath record?

—Ha.

—I don't care. Put something on. What you got?

—New Black Sabbath.

—Seriously.

—I don't know. I just got Miles' *Sketches from Spain* on CD.

—Good, I haven't heard that in a while.

—Ok then.

*

—Like Richard Nixon, I was born in a house my father built, a basement he poured. A sandlot diamond behind the house where I got a splinter once in my rear. The bigger boys laughed. A street of gravel with ditches for drainage: Eighth Street. And a cocker spaniel bitch named Cyrano. I was born with eyes the color of the sea, green and mud, a dull roiling behind a semitranslucent screen. Born in a matter of minutes, so fast the nurses were dubious, the doctor almost late.

The town was Lewiston, New York, a carbuncle on the gritty side of gritty Niagara Falls, New York, the former honeymoon capital of the United States, a country which, like Niagara Falls in microcosm, had lately fallen into disrepair. Now, Niagara Falls, Ontario, just over the national border, where my mother's incredibly large family hailed from, was bright and brisk and clean and gardeny, the shiny flipside of its American counterpart.

I longed to be from the Canadian side; I longed to be Canadian. I thought my mother's family was just about the most exotic thing I could imagine (and later in school I used her heritage as if it were some bizarre ethnic upbringing, as if one side of my family tree was hung with Hottentots, or Eskimos), and my Canuck uncles, who were all big, strapping, lumberjack men, who could hold seven or eight nieces and nephews on their back, were the ideal of manhood with which I constantly compared my scrawny, allergic, weak-wristed self (no upper body strength, my tennis coach would later tell me).

Actually I have few memories from Lewiston. We left there when I was five, my father worked for DuPont de Nemours and Company and followed their natural trade route to Memphis, Tennessee, in the spring of 1960. What memories I do possess are clouded as if suspended in aspic, dream recollections, impressionistic and shadowy. I remember Cyrano. (A car hit him? He died of old age? At any rate he was gone before our move south). I vaguely remember the baseball diamond. I remember comparing peepees with the girl down the street; I even remember her name (well, of course I do, my first sex, my first glimpse behind the door of esotericism) which was Sandy. I remember, as if from a bad dream, a life lesson dream, getting a hellacious shock from our electric football game. This was a flat metal gameboard which you plugged into the wall and it vibrated and your defensive and offensive formations danced together (or apart) in random, chaotic tremblings, until the player with the ball (a small plastic chip) was shaken off the playing field. I think I piled rubber bricks on the game (although rubber shouldn't give you a shock, should it?) and was jolted into an acute awareness, which obviously left its impression. I believe this is my clearest memory of Lewiston: a healthy dose of 120 volts.

My big brother, Mark, was 11 or 12 when we moved; my little sister, Susan (Sue), would have been a babe in arms. Kindergarten in Lewiston I remember as traumatic (separation from Mother) and painful (my fingers were smashed in the car door one frosty morning by my rambunctious cousin John), and humiliating (the lesson early: do not use the school restroom, hold it and begin a life of lower intestinal disorders).

Moved to a city beside a great rolling river, the color of my eyes at dusk, mud flecked with green. A city of irony and pity, a Bluff City. Memphis, Tennessee, where this action and inaction takes place.

*

—So, you know I've been having these tests for food allergies.
—Yeah.
—Turns out I'm allergic to coffee.
—Weird.
—Well, weird enough. Not that weird, really. I'm allergic so far to everything they've tested me for. But, listen. Coffee. I mean, it's one of my few genuine pleasures. You know, I think people who love coffee, like Dorothea and myself, are also passionate about life. It's just a theory, mind you, but I feel like the person who sits over a warm, humbling beverage and breathes it in, and enjoys, you know, fixing it, unfolding the filter, grinding the beans, pouring hot water over them, the whole process—and life is relishing the processes, isn't it? —well, that person is somehow attached to the world in a really adjoined, meaningful way.

—Didn't you have this same theory about changing diapers?

—Yes, exactly. Another time, though. Coffee, it's a simple pleasure, a moment in the day to be relished for its intelligible, uncomplicated significance. Sitting in the morning, with my scone and my newspaper, it's reaffirming, you know. And it has to have all three components for accomplishment, to have power: coffee (in our beloved bowl-sized mugs), scone (I can settle for some 7-grain toast, an English muffin), newspaper. It's especially meaningful on Sundays with that big fat paper full of worthy and worthless items—I find myself pouring over the hiring of a basketball coach at Georgia Tech, or how a St. Jude physician came to Memphis from Zimbabwe. But to have those things, there, on my lap of a morning, it can feel, temporarily, like *the whole*. I feel attached.

—Not a common thing in life.

—Right. So, to find I'm allergic to coffee, well, it's everything in a nutshell, isn't it? It's emblematic of the whole.

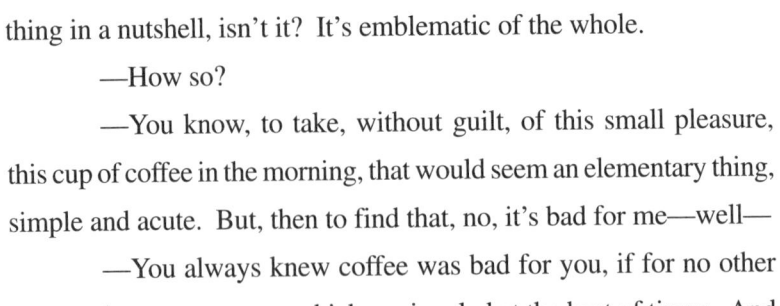

—How so?

—You know, to take, without guilt, of this small pleasure, this cup of coffee in the morning, that would seem an elementary thing, simple and acute. But, then to find that, no, it's bad for me—well—

—You always knew coffee was bad for you, if for no other reason, than your nerves, which are jangled at the best of times. And your intestines, coffee, I think I read somewhere, disturbs those delicate linings which abet the flow of food from nourishment to waste to excreta.

—Thank you. Yes, but to have it medically justified, you know, it's—it's emblematic. I cannot partake of the smallest joy.

—You think you're, what, what's Woody Allen's word?

—Anhedonic.

—Right. Is that you? Can you really not appreciate anything?

—It's true enough to remark upon. Anhedonic. Well, sure, I mean, I look at my laughing daughter and concentrate on her pealing cackles, and I think, I'm enjoying the laughter of my daughter.

—That's good, though.

—No, not really. It's so self-conscious. I mean, the next moment I could be thinking, I don't really enjoy this, or this simple pleasure is also denied me.

—Jesus, Jim. You're what, projecting. Live in the moment is not a credo you even consider, is it?

—No. I can't. I really can't.

*

—Hey, Princess.

—Daddy, I'm gonna get a new new new new—kitten.

—Really.

—A white one.

—White would be pretty.

—Madison has a black kitty.

—Uh huh.

—And I'm gonna get a white kitty.

—Sure. What's Madison's kitty's name?

—And a new new new alligator.

—An alligator?

—Yeah. And Madison said *Po* and Flannery said *Doug*.

—Ok. Oh, for the name of the fish at daycare?

—Yeah.

—And what do you want to call your white kitty?

—Um. Tinky Winky.

—That's a good name.

—And Madison calls her kitty *Oreo*.

—That's a pretty good name for a black kitty.

—Uh huh. Cuz he's black.

—Like an Oreo.

—Uh huh.

—Where did you see an alligator?

—At the pet store.

—Oh. Did you pet him?

—He won't hurt you. Alligators don't bite you.

—Ok.

—He's nice.

—Ok.

—I'm gonna get an alligator and a blue parrot and a snake.

—A snake? I thought snakes were yuck.

—Um. Yeah, snakes are yuck. I'm gonna name my alligator, um—

—What? Lyle.

—Nao. Um, Tinky Winky.

—Ha. Ok. You know when Connie was little he named everything *BooBoo*. We had a frog named BooBoo and a couple of stuffed toys named BooBoo and I forget whatall.

—We don't have a frog.

—No, we don't anymore.

—We don't keep frogs as pets.

—Ok. Ok, Princess.

*

—Hey.

—Mr. In and Out.

—So to speak.

—I wish so to speak.

—Um.

—Sorry. Come in. You wanna a Diet Dr. Pepper?

—Ooh, fancy.

—I got other things. Uh, club soda. I think I've got one chocolate soldier.

—What am I, twelve? Glass of club soda please.

—You want it in a glass. I'll have to wash one.

—Right. No, just cold from the bottle, like the college boys drink it.

—I don't think I have a cold one.

—How about ice. You got ice?

—Lemme check. I got a cube.

—One cube. It'll do. You run a tight ship here.

—Very funny. I live alone, bucko. I please myself.

—I know.

—So.

—Thanks.

—What's up? This a social call, or have you anything of major import to impart.

—Import to impart, pretty good.

—Thanks. You think you're the only wordsmith round these parts?

—No. Um, just a social call, I guess. Missed you, felt guilty about missing you, overrode the guilt, got horny, more guilt, more but stronger overriding need, and so on.

—Hm. I'm flattered and flummoxed.

—Just the way I like you.

—And you do like me?

—Yes. Yes, I do.

—Hm. I like you, too.

—Established.

—Ok. Now what.

—You wanna play cards.

—I've got my period.

—So you can't play cards?

—No. I thought you meant, you know—

—I know, I'm just teasing.

—Right. You really want to play cards?

—No.

—Watch TV?

—You got cable?

—No. I don't watch much TV.

—Forget it.

—Your ice has melted.

—So it has.

—You want to kiss me?

—Yes.

—Mmm. That's good. I should have brushed my teeth.

—No, no. It was fine.

—There's an endorsement. You sound real enthusiastic. Fine.

—No, I mean your breath. Your kiss was tender and delectable as usual.

—Ok.

—Another?

—Sure.

*

—My children, wife, dog, extended family, obviously.
—Yes.
—Um, friends.
—Thank you.
—Assuredly. Humor, of course, self-irony, I think we've agreed. Food, Dylan, The Beatles. Books, books, books—more specifically, um, Updike, Sweet Iris Murdoch, Wodehouse, Barth, Joyce, um—
—Roth.
—O yes. *Little, Big.* Yeats, Mark Strand, Dr. Seuss...
—Ha. Enough. Books, granted.
—*Lolita.*
—Ok.
—Movies. Shall we do specifics? Woody Allen, Fellini, Bergman.
—Those three are enough, surely.
—A holy triumvirate. *Children of Paradise, The Day the Earth Stood Still.*
—Yes.
—*Spinal Tap.* Ok. Ice cream. The beach.
—You don't like to travel.
—Can't travel. A sad irony, isn't it? Still, love the beach. There's something very soothing about the lapping, etc. of the waves, something deep about the impenetrable water, the odor, its funk, its brack, its unfathomable color like a smeared palette, a mix of all color, its seeming limitlessness, so murky, so mysterious.

—All puns intended.

—Oh, deep, ha yes. Music.

—Tertiary to books and movies?

—That's a hard one. Let's not rank. Let's rank elsewhere. Music.

—Though you already said Dylan and the Beatles.

—Well. Dylan and the Beatles transcend even the category. They are touchstones.

—I know.

—And maybe Leonard Cohen. Another holy trio.

—Ok.

—Love, sex, men and women together. Romance. I mean is there anything more charming, more sustaining than those connections, that buzz between two attached people.

—I don't know. I've always found other people's love to be, what, annoying.

—Like something you don't quite believe in. Yeah, you're right. I guess I'm concentrating on selfish categories here. That connection for me, I guess. Love that sex pull.

—Right.

—How about that first time you read a book you know is going to end up being important to you? That's a magical feeling. That's an affirmation that there's more to man than chemicals and electrons.

—You've already said books.

—Subcategory.

—Ok.

—Dogs. Babies. There's something apersonal. I get a hum in my heart for most babies, anyone's. You look at them, they meet your eyes, it's—beyond understanding, supernatural. A real world feeling, you know, a link.

—And dogs, too?

—In a way. You ever look a dog in the face and it stares back and then it blinks its eyes? Do that. Blink at a dog and it'll blink back. There's something there.

—You know dog spelled backwards—

—Funny. Go ahead and scoff at my profundity.

—No no. I'm a big fan of your profundity, as you know.

—All right. To continue. Writing. When I used to. Selling books, when it's right. Not, you know, shelving and reshelving the current tell-alls, or looking up some mundane college text book, not fetching from high on the back shelves another copy of *Refrigeration and Air Conditioning, 3rd Edition,* but that rapport with a real reader, who wants something as good as, say, Bruno Schulz. That's a kick that's more moving than it should be. Selling a good novel, knowing that person is about to enter a magical realm, say, take home and fall into *The Philosopher's Pupil* for the first time, you know, just discover some book which you have taken to heart, which, perhaps has affected you deeply, changed you utterly, a terrible beauty being born. Ok. *The Simpsons. The Dick Van Dyke Show.* My mother's spaghetti. *Twilight Zone. Monty Python. Looney Tunes.* The smell of bacon in the morning. Our house full of our things. Going out onto the porch in the early morning when there's a little nip in the air, feeling the cool boards of the porch on bare feet. Something about that makes me feel alive.

—A good thing.

—Basketball, when it's well played.

—Basketball, when it's poorly played.

—Second only to basketball when it's well played. Games, playing Scrabble with Connie, or Monopoly. Or Trivial Pursuit, which is not one.

—All good things.

—What have we left out?

—Birds and birdsong. Infinity, though it scares me.

—Define.

—You know, looking up into the endlessness of the sky, wondering about the imponderable: does the universe have an end, and if so what's beyond that. Knowing there's a limit to human understanding.

—You sound religious.

—Yes.

—What else?

—I don't know. Taco Bell.

—Ok.

—That's about it, I guess.

—Enough.

—Yes.

—So, we go on living?

—For now.

*

—Kids asleep?

—Yes.

—Katey's cough any better?

—Oh, yeah. She's tough, you know. Tough as Connie. Tough little immune systems our children have.

—Which is a blessing.

—Yes, indeed.

—My favorite part of the day. When the house has settled down, when there's only the low-level burble of the TV or the sound of light rain on the roof. You know you've got your family safe and tucked in and the comfort of sleep is theirs. I love that alone time, feeling the peace of being settled, there's nothing else as comforting.

—You want me to go to bed and leave you to it.

—No no. Come a little bit closer.

—Mm.

—You smell good. Your hair smells good.

—You feel good.

—Good.

—You want to go to bed? You want to fool around?

—In a minute.

—This is nice enough.

—Yes.

—Though a little tumble might feel good, too.

—Oh, yes.

—Kiss me.

—You have a wonderful waist, my hand just there.

—Thank you.

—Mm. Kiss me again.

—Nice. Your breath tastes of licorice.

—I hate licorice.

—Nevertheless.

—You have wonderful thighs, too. So soft. And a flower between your legs.

—The things you say.

—Is that Katey coughing?

—I think that's Fly. Relax.

—Yes.

—Kiss me again.

—Ok.

*

—Hello?

—

—Hi Mom.

—

—Nothing. Fixing to go to work. Anything wrong?

—

—No, it's just odd for you to call this early.

—

—Been up that long, huh?

—

—I'm sorry.

—

—Everyone's fine. Connie's got a project due today, so we're trying to get everything together here.

—

—No, I didn't mean that. It's just clumsy trying to carry a posterboard in with that ninety-pound backpack they make the kids tote these days.

—

—No, not literally ninety pounds.

—

—We're all fine, honest.

—

—Dorothea's fine, she's right here. You wanna talk to her?

—

—Ok. We're fine. Happy as clams.

—

—I don't know why clams are happy, Ma. Everything alright there?

—

—I know he snores. He makes up for it during the day by being a loyal and attentive husband.

—

—Just kidding, or something. Just being light.

—

—Oh. Well. Oh, I love you, too.

—

—Ok, Ma.

—

—Right. Bye-bye.

*

—You masturbate much?

—Oh boy.

—Really, a lot?

—No, I mean, oh boy, this conversation's starting on a high plane.

—Don't want to talk about it?

—I don't know. What's much?

—Compared to, say, the early 20s.

—Well, then, no. Decidedly, no.

—Really?

—Yeah. Why? You?

—Sure. Once a day.

—Really? In the confines of marriage.

—Oh, be realistic. Maybe a little less.

—Yeah?

—You don't?

—Oh, if I'm going through a particularly horny time. Seen too many Gap ads, that sort of thing. Ginger going through one of her periodic down times, which, as you know, can be lengthy. Then sure. But in a good cycle, during a normal healthily sexual time, no, gotta save it for the wife.

—Oh sure. I don't do it on a day when Dorothea and I are gonna, you know.

—You have a schedule?

—Practically. No. Not really. But with kids—

—I know. I don't know though. I figure I've only got so much jism in me, God has granted me x number of orgasms, see. And I don't want to waste too many of them on my own tired old palm.

—Yeah, sure. But then, if we only have x number, I don't plan on dying with any still in the bank.

—Ha. Right.

*

—You sounded bad on the phone. Everything all right?

—Yes. Come in.

—Thank you. You sound so formal.

—Sorry. Sit here.

—Ok.

—You okay?

—Yes, fine. What is it?

—Nothing, really. Just missed you, goddamit.

—Sorry.

—You're sorry.

—Well, I mean—

—Damn, Jim. I'm sorry. I'm not this way, really.

—What way is that?

—Whiny. Manipulative.

—I've never thought of you that way.

—It's just—I don't know. I'm having a vulnerable day, I guess.

—Certainly an ok thing.

—Thanks.

—I guess this is gonna be one of those I can't say anything right times.

—No. Sorry. Come here.

—I'm right here.

—Hold me.

—Yes.

—You doing all right? Everything ok at home, at work?

—Sure, sure.

—Talk to me.

—Ok. Um. Held a first edition of Fitzgerald's *Great Gatsby* in my hands today. Signed.

—Wow.

—I know. It was Fitzgerald's signature. He signed it. That page right in front of me.

—You buy it?

—Wanted to. Couldn't come to an agreement.

—Oh well.

—Yeah, oh well. Seemed enough to just hold it, though. You know? I'm not sure I wanted it to be just a piece of commerce, somehow. Just wanted to relish it.

—You sell first editions for a living, lunkhead.

—I know. I need to improve my perspective.

—What else?

—Um. Connie has a science project.

—On what?

—Do you really want to make small talk?

—Is it small talk to discuss your kids?

—No, of course not.

—I am really interested, you know. I *do* care about your children, you know.

—Ok.

—Ok.

—Um.

—Damn, I'm sorry. Maybe you ought to go.

—Ok.

—Sorry.

—It's ok.

*

—How's it going, Marco?

—All right. Ginger might be pregnant.

—Jesus. This is earthshattering. This is fantastic. Why didn't you tell me?

—Well, we just sort of figured it out this afternoon and I knew I'd see you tonight.

—Wow.

—Besides we don't want to talk about it too much yet. It's so unsure. She's doing a pregnancy test tonight while I'm out.

—Man. You didn't want to be there?

—Sure. She didn't want me to be. Said I might jinx it.

—Women have some funny ideas. Gotta respect them, though.

—Yes.

—You'll of course let me know as soon—

—Yes. Listen, there's something else.

—Uh oh. Don't like that tone.

—Katya said something to me today at work.

—Shit.

—Yeah. She just out of the blue said she had been seeing you.

—Seeing me? That's what she said?

—Yes. Which she quickly amended. Said, well, you had just dropped by a few times.

—Oh, man.

—So what's going on, Jimbo? I mean for her to bring it up to me—

—Means she's obsessing a bit, perhaps. Means it means something.

—Yes.

—Time to nip it in the bud.

—I think so.

—Me, too. God knows I don't need it.

—What? Don't need what?

—Any of it. Complications. Pain. Even extra sex.

—Ok then.

—I'll stop. I don't think a conference with her is in order, do you? I mean, I think if I just let it drop, don't call, don't go by, it'll just sort of drift into history. Fade away. Let it evaporate, ay?

—I don't know.

—You counsel the face to face?

—I think so. It's cleaner.

—I don't know. I'll think about it.

—Ok.

—But this about Ginger. Wow. This is major.

—I hope so. Don't talk about it yet.

—Right.

*

—Hi.

—Come in.

—Hi.

—Hi. Ok?

—Yes. You look great.

—Thank you.

—Those are very short shorts.

—Yes they are. I didn't expect company.

—Nevertheless, those look great on you.

—Thanks.

—You okay?

—Sure.

—Good.

—What's up?

—Nothing. Wanted to see you.

—You seem, what, nervous.

—I guess I am.

—This the final tête-à-tête?

—I guess.

—Ok.

—Katya.

—It's ok, really. I need to move on.

—Yes.

—So, is that it?

—Not so abruptly. I mean.

—I said it's ok. No guilt.

—Well—

—Sorry, I forgot I was talking to Franz Kafka.

—Thanks.

—It's ok, Jim.

—Ok.

—You want some lemonade.

—You know I do.

—Ok.

—Your butt looks good in those shorts.

—Thank you. Stop looking at it.

—Right.

—It's not homemade.

—Your butt?

—Funny man.

—Yep.

—It's Crystal Light.

—Fine.

—What's new in Jimville?

—Nothing. Absolutely nothing.

—Hm.

—Great news about Ginger isn't it?

—What?

—Oh, shit. Nothing.

—She's pregnant?

—They're not sure. I don't think I was supposed to say anything. Shit. Mums the word, ok?

—Sure.

—You don't have a bra on?

—That was a wild segue.

—Sorry, I just noticed. That T-shirt is so loose.

—You're feeling randy for a fellow intent on a brush-off.

—Yes. Sorry.

—That's ok. It's all ok.

—That's a wonderful thing about you, that it's all ok.

—Yep.

—

—

—What are you doing?

—Well, I'm running my hand over my breasts through my T-shirt.

—I see.

—I might be fending off your salvo. I might be forestalling the inevitable, distracting you, trying to hold on to you a little longer. Maybe just pushing the envelope. Maybe making one last grab for your attention, wanting to end on a bang, so to speak, instead of a whimper. Give you something to remember me by.

—Oh, Katya.

—And it feels good.

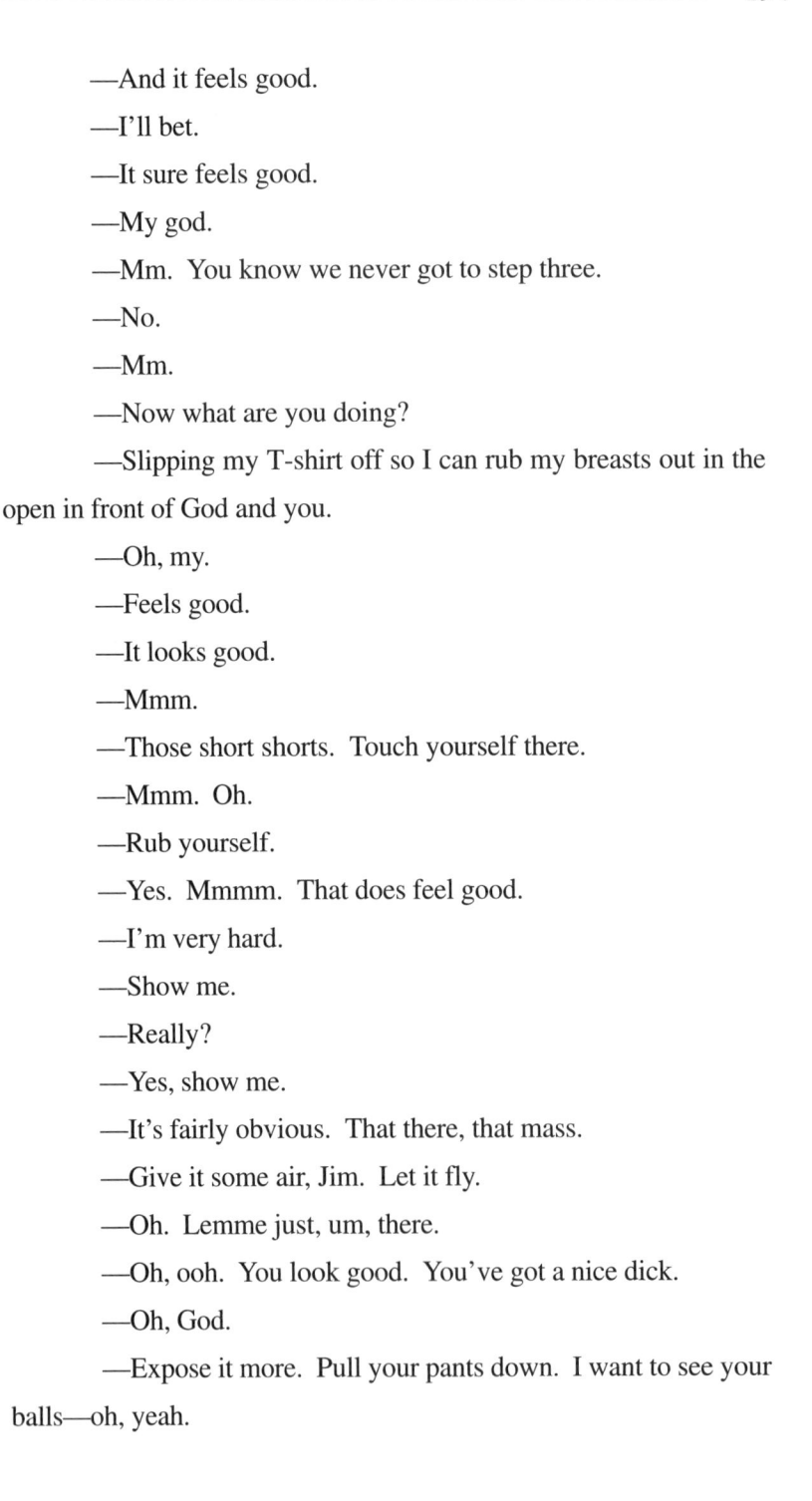

—I'll bet.

—It sure feels good.

—My god.

—Mm. You know we never got to step three.

—No.

—Mm.

—Now what are you doing?

—Slipping my T-shirt off so I can rub my breasts out in the open in front of God and you.

—Oh, my.

—Feels good.

—It looks good.

—Mmm.

—Those short shorts. Touch yourself there.

—Mmm. Oh.

—Rub yourself.

—Yes. Mmmm. That does feel good.

—I'm very hard.

—Show me.

—Really?

—Yes, show me.

—It's fairly obvious. That there, that mass.

—Give it some air, Jim. Let it fly.

—Oh. Lemme just, um, there.

—Oh, ooh. You look good. You've got a nice dick.

—Oh, God.

—Expose it more. Pull your pants down. I want to see your balls—oh, yeah.

—My. You.

—What?

—Unzip those obscenely short shorts. Yes.

—There, Jim. There.

—Yes. I love those panties.

—Mmm. I'm taking them off.

—Oh, God. You're naked. You're completely naked.

—I am. Yes.

—Oh, touch it more. More.

—Mmm. Mm, God. Take your pants all the way off. Yes.

—Open your thighs. Oh, God.

—Oh, oh. Oh that feels good.

—I—I

—I like—ah—looking at your cock while I masturbate. Stroke it harder.

—Ah—ahh

—Oh, Jim, yeah. I want it, oh God, it looks so good—

—Jesus, Katya, Jesus. Oh—

—Jim—I—

—Yes, do it. Come. Let it go—

—Ah—ahhhhh

—Oh, Katya—

—Oh, oh mmmm

—That was good. That was good, wasn't it?

—Mmm.

—Oh, Katya.

—Now you.

—We don't have to.

—I know. Do it.

—Oh—

—Do you want me to touch myself some more? Like that? Look, look, Jim.

—Oh, yes. Oh—

—Do it Jim.

—Yes.

—Jim.

—Mmm

—Jim, I want to suck it. Please.

—Oh, my God, yes, oh my—

—Oh, Jim. Mmmm.

*

—I know. There is pain.

And there is pain and there are nightquakes and there is still, even in the midst of such loving togetherness, such solid *consistency* as Dorothea and I have attained, there is still the flesh-loneliness, the need. What kind of plan is that? Isn't happiness, contentedness proof against anything. It's impotent. It's like a cellophane barrier. So weak, transparent, almost no one believes in it. I don't believe in it. I want and I want and I want. And hate myself for that. Having much doesn't abort the need. The sad desideratum. It is how it is. Yet. This is wrong, cellularly, chromosonally wrong. I know this. This, at least, I know.

*

—Hey, big guy.

—Dad, I want to write.

—Ok. What do you want to write?

—I don't know. Poems.

—Good choice.

—What do I write about?

—Oh, anything. Poems can be about anything. That's one of the glories of poems. You ever hear this game, TEGWAR? T-E-G-W-A-R. It stands for "The exciting game without any rules." A good enough job description for a poet.

—Yeah, but what can I write about?

—Um. I don't know, Con. What interests you, what concerns you?

—There's this girl in my class.

—Now you're talking. One of the prime motivators of poets throughout time.

—Well, I think she goes with someone else.

—Ouch. What do you mean, goes with?

—You know.

—Yes.

—I could write about Fly.

—Sure. You want to write a poem to this girl?

—I don't know.

—Afraid someone might find out?

—Yeah.

—Well, write it and just keep it to yourself. The important thing, the first step, is writing it.

—Yeah.

—Love is a large subject, big as the sky.

—I don't love her.

—Well, no.

—I could write about Katey.

—That would be nice.

—I drew her something. I drew her a Teletubbie.

—I know. I saw it. She showed it to me. She was very proud of it.

—Maybe I'll write her a poem.

—Katey?

—Naw, this girl in my class. Belle.

—Whoa. That's her name, Belle?

—Yeah.

—You got a lot to deal with there, buddy.

—What do you mean?

—Nothing. Go for it.

—Maybe.

—Lemme know. Ok?

*

—Hey, Katiegirl. Hey, Shortstack.
—Sit in you lap.
—I'd love it. Come up here.
—I can't play with Uncle Max's dog.
—No?
—He might bite me.
—Well. You have to be careful.
—But I can play with Uncle Max.
—Sure. Ha, of course.
—But Titus might bite.
—Right.
—Halloween's gonna come again.
—Yes. It is.
—And Thanksgiving and New Years and Valentimes Day.
—Uh huh.
—And Christmas. Christmas is gonna come again.
—Right.
—And I'm gonna get lots of presents.
—All right.
—And Valentimes Day is gonna come again.
—They're all gonna come again, sweetheart. And again and again.
—And Halloween.
—Yes, Halloween again. Time and time again. Amen.

*

—Hello?

—

—Oh, hi.

—

—Yes, well.

—

—I'm sorry, do I?

—

—It's just that, you know. We went too far.

—

—I know it's ok. It's just—

—

—No. I mean, yes, I'm feeling guilty. It's just—

—

—No, we went too far.

—

—No, just, I don't know how to say this. We went too far and I don't want to do that again.

—

—Right. I guess so.

—

—No. I can't. Again.

—

—Ever.

—

—I guess so. I guess that is what I'm saying.

—

—I'm sorry.

—

—I know.

—

—I know. It's all right.

—

—I know it's all ok.

—

—Thank you.

—

—No just for—you know.

—

—For you.

—

—Yes.

—

—Ok.

*

—Where's Connie?
—At Ethan's, I think.
—Should we worry that we often don't know where he is?

—Naw. He's a big boy, now.

—I know. Hard to let go, isn't it? Hard to strike that balance. He's between Man and Boy. Yesterday he was walking through the living room singing a Green Day song, holding a stuffed Super Mario. There it was nutshelled for me. Slash and burn punk music and a stuffed toy.

—Yeah.

—Hard to strike any balances really.

—What's that mean?

—I don't know. Nothing.

—Hey. Ginger called. She's pregnant.

—Whoa. Great. I knew, actually.

—What do you mean you knew? Why didn't you tell me?

—I mean, I thought she was. Mark said they thought so. Didn't want me to say anything to anyone yet, till they were sure.

—I'm your wife.

—I know. Sorry. It just sort of never came up. I'm glad though. Wonder why that jackass didn't call me.

—They're thrilled.

—I bet.

—Never thought of Mark that way though.

—Whaddya mean?

—As a father. Settled down.

—Really?

—Yeah. I always thought Mark was a bit of a stray cat, a ladies' man.

—You're kidding.

—No, why would I kid?

—I don't know. Mark's like the fucking Rock of Gibraltar.

He's the goddammed Heaven's snowy flake.

   —Ok. Don't get so heated. I thought, I don't know, you know that wispy blond he works with?

   —Um, yeah.

   —I just thought, you know, he had a thing for her.

   —Jesus, Dorothea. Mark's like a saint. He's like the conscience of his generation.

   —Ok.

   —He's like butter wouldn't melt in his mouth. It's like he stands in the rain and doesn't get wet.

   —Ok. *Ok.* Christ.

   —All right.

   —Anyway, great for them, eh?

   —Yes.

   —Ok.

   —I better call him.

*

   —Hi. Can I help you?

   —Um.

   —Anything in particular?

   —I need. Um.

   —

   —Uh.

—Do you know the title?

—I—

—Maybe the author. I can look it up—

—Um.

—Any word in the title? What's it about?

—It's. It was on—

—I'm sorry I can barely hear you.

—It was—

—Oprah?

—No. Um—

—You saw it on TV?

—Yeah. Yes.

—You don't remember the title?

—No. Um. I don't care which title. Um.

—

—It's about—

—

—Um. How to. Um.

—

—Feel better.

—

—About. Yourself.

*

—So, don't tell me you and the wife are having bedroom problems again?

—Oh, yeah.

—Damn.

—I think she just has a low libido. She has a libido set on, like, two.

—Some women do. Some don't, thank God.

—Well. I also get the idea she uses her period for extended vacations. It used to keep us from having sex one to two day, tops. Now, it's a week. Ten days.

—Uh oh.

—Exactly. I mean I don't like the injustice of the menses, as you know. I voted against it.

—There you go. You're a just man.

—It's not fair.

—It's not.

—Well, anyway. I still love her, God knows I do.

—Yes.

—But, sex, Sweet Jesus.

—Don't want to quit that game yet.

—Nope.

—Don't blame you.

—Maybe it's me. I've put on some weight—

—Hey. Buddy. I'd fuck you. If, you know, you were a woman.

—Thanks.

*

—No matter how diffuse, how splintered your life becomes, it all adds up. Even if you don't want it to, even if you don't care. In the end there is a pattern, one that no one could predict, one that encompasses all the errors, all the wrong turns, all the fucking up we go through. In the end, pure or simple or complex or ugly it all adds up and you're left with, what, something still unformed. I guess that's what I want to say. The pattern you make, the pot you form with all this manifold clay, ends up, ugly or beautiful, a still ragged piece of work. But there it is. Ugly and finalized. I don't know. You try to figure anything out and even if you can come up with some kind of solution, it's incomplete. There is a sum, but you feel that it's not your sum, or that the sum doesn't explain anything. Dorothea is a great problem solver. Give her a dilemma and her mind immediately begins to work on a resolution, it's just the way she's made. She is empirical. She believes that in *Star Trek* no matter how screwed up things became, how complexly bad, they were right to search for and find a solution every hour. By the end of each episode it was meet and right that there was a settlement. Normally, you know, it involved locating the power source and negating it, even if that meant negating matter itself. But it was just. It was what was *supposed* to happen. The idiom of empiricism is alive in my capable and determined wife. And she's right because that works for her. She really can find ways to make life better, to make it less stressful, less complicated. And it's not that she's a shallow person, far from it. She is wonderfully intricate and exciting, but she firmly assumes that life's tangle, given the right amount of intelligence and acute action applied to it, can be unraveled. God bless her. It is one of the things I love about her. But it's not me. And she is a font of patience and wisdom when faced with my disbelief. I am easily defeated by the simplest tasks; I stand outside the simplest calms. I am an agnostic about the solution, about where this all leads, where this all gets sewn up. I want to believe, I do. But I am made of weaker stuff. Sometimes I am not even confident enough to get out of bed. But I do it, of course. I do it for her, for the children. And, selfishly, for me, too. To see what a new day can offer, what pleasure just *might* come my way. I seek pleasure. Sorry, but I do. Life's too depressing if you don't. I can't face the day if you take away my coffee. Call me ineffectual: I am made of flimsy, insubstantial material.

I am gypsum and gum. I am abstraction, too much abstraction.

It's a story after all, isn't it. The story of someone not having an affair, of someone coming this close to having an affair, of someone having or not having the affair, the line between the situational moralities we construct, the story of the silence which surrounds all of that, all of us.

I fling this into that silence, hoping to shatter it, end it, without hope, looking for hope. I fling this into the eternal silence that surrounds us all.

It's all I know to do. Talk.

—

—Sometimes I think I will get an answer. Sometimes not.

—

—Some days I feel competent, like I can handle the world, anything the world wants to toss my way, broken headlight, poopy diaper, the sadness of one's significant other, the open-ended sadness which has nothing to do with anything except that it is hard, *hard* to be human. Some days I will feel barbarously not competent.

I feel good. I feel bad. I take a pill in between. E. M. Cioran said, "The more one hates Man, the riper one is for God, for a dialogue with nobody." I don't hate Man.

—

—In psychiatry they call it the *talking cure*. I want to believe. I want to believe it all works. I want it to work and for a God to see it all and think that it is good and that there is a plan and that plan includes even our pitiful attempts at connection, is, perhaps made of those attempts. I want that. That dialogue.

—

—I want to talk about it. If only for me, just to talk about it.

—

—

—If anyone is there to listen.

—

—You're whispering. I can't hear you.
—Jim. Shh, Jim.

Photograph: © 2001 Irma C. Idell

COREY MESLER is the co-owner of Burke's Book Store, in Memphis, Tennessee, one of the country's oldest (127 years) and best independent bookstores. He has published poetry and fiction in numerous journals including *Yellow Silk, Pindeldyboz, Green Egg, Black Dirt, Thema, Mars Hill Review, Poet Lore*. He has worked in the book business all his adult life, if he has had an adult life. He has also been a book reviewer for *The Memphis Commercial Appeal, The Memphis Flyer, Brightleaf* and *BookPage*. He's been a pirate, a pauper, a puppet, a poet, a pawn and a king. A short story of his has been chosen for the 2002 edition of *New Stories from the South: The Year's Best*, edited by Shannon Ravenel, published by Algonquin Books. He also claims to have written, "All Along the Watchtower." *Talk* is his first novel. He is now at work on a collection of linked stories, built from poorly remembered history and bent mythology. Most importantly, he is Toby and Chloe's dad and Cheryl's husband.